St. Louis Lucifer

How I Danced with the Devil in the Midwest Moonlight

Victoria L. Szulc

DISCLAIMER: Although there are references to actual events, places, and people, some names have been changed to protect the innocent, timelines are not in direct order, and conversations are edited and paraphrased for brevity. This work is based on a true story.

Cover Photography/Art Direction: Victoria L. Szulc
Cover Design: Michele Berhorst

Credit to: "The Last Lemp" by Jeanette Cooperman, May 15, 2015, St. Louis Magazine.

ISBN: 978-1-958760-46-8

DEDICATION

To my sister Lisa who finally found her way out of darkness and into angels' arms.

PREFACE

"Did you ever fart in anyone's face?" Andrew Barringer* asked me as we drove through the 64/Market Street merge near Downtown West St. Louis. I burst into incredulous laughter, barely able to breathe and drive as I aligned his shiny black Mercedes with other cars getting onto the highway. I continued to chortle for at least another minute until I pulled off at the 22nd street exit with a grand view of the St. Louis Wheel, Union Station, and the Downtown skyline radiating in the late day sun. My answer was no, his answer was yes, in case you were wondering.

That was one of our fabulous Sunday drives where we visited antique malls, cruised around historic homes and parks, picking in the bins at Goodwill, and getting QuikTrip pizza before heading back to a historic house museum where I was weekend manager and caretaker. We talked about his famous and infamous family members, many of which helped found the very fiber of the Gateway to the West. We reminisced about our families, art, history, books, and movies with plenty of double entendres, jokes, and serious recollections sprinkled in. I will always wonder how many of those adventurous moments were authentic, because six months later, I'd discover that Andrew Barringer was far from the person he claimed to be.

For over a year, I was in an intimate friendship with a tall, dark, and handsome man named Andrew. One I manifested, although I should have been more specific and asked the universe to send me a straight man. This is my story of the time we spent together and how he manipulated his way back into the region's cultural and historical institutions from which he had been banished only ten years earlier.

**Author's note to the reader: because Andrew victimized so many innocent people, organizations, and businesses, along with his extensive lies and claims, I have chosen to change the names of certain people and places in this book.*

DISCLAIMER: Although there are references to actual events, places, and people, some names have been changed to protect the innocent, timelines are not in direct order, and conversations are edited and paraphrased for brevity.

CONTENTS

ACKNOWLEDGMENTS

Thank you to my family, friends, and readers who have supported me and this work. Special thanks to the others affected by Andrew that bravely came forward to share their stories.

1 MEET THE DEVIL

"No wonder, for even Satan disguises himself as an angel of light."
-Corinthians 11:14

June 2024

"What kind of men do you like? What's your type?" I inquire as Andrew and I drive around like we often do. We'd been friends for a couple of weeks and the conversation came easily with silly often crude jokes and shocking admissions thrown in.

"Married," he says it in such a deadpan way that I guffaw aloud.

"Really?"

"Straight on the down low is even better." He smirks behind classic dark designer sunglasses. His quips and quick attention-getting tactics started not long after we'd begun hanging out a month before.

When I recall how easily I'd fallen into the belief of Andrew's deceptions, I see that I was ripe for the picking. I'd had a really rough several years, especially in the autumn into winter seasons.

A few years ago, my father passed away. I developed a severe tooth infection during year two of the Covid pandemic when getting in to see a dentist was nearly impossible. The next autumn, I fell and contused my knee after a ten-hour shift of baking at work. The bruise went to the bone and lasted for eight weeks. My pain was a huge distraction.

Six months earlier in March 2024, I'd just decided to "retire" from being the caretaker of the grand Campbell House Museum after over five years of service. My term was set to end in March of the next year, 2025. I lived blissfully in the carriage house, enjoying a historic oasis that inspired my fictional writing and other creative arts.

It was a sunny mid-June day when I had to run and check my mail at the Museum's break room. I wasn't inside the gift shop door but a minute, when an attractive man strode down the disabled ramp leading a tour group. He had a volunteers lanyard but I hadn't met him before. He wore an oxford style dress shirt and tan colored trousers embroidered with charming little mallard ducks. He tugged them up in the way that men do when it's been a long day and adjustments needed to be made for comfort in the tummy. He had thick shiny black hair sprouting touches of grey, and a matching well-trimmed beard and mustache.

Although it was early afternoon, I was exhausted. I was a baker for my "day job" at the time, either working early morning or very late, writing and doing pop up shops and art shows when I was able. I should get my mail and go, but something told me I needed to find out about this new volunteer. Of course, I found him attractive, nearly everyone thought he was. His charm was infectious. I sensed he was gay, although straight acting.

I paused to talk to a volunteer working the gift shop as he moved guests forward. I looked like absolute shit, wearing an old beat up tee shirt and leggings. I was hoping I wouldn't run into anyone, but I introduced myself anyway.

"Hi, are you a new volunteer? I'm Victoria, the caretaker and weekend manager of the Museum."

"Oh, I'm Andrew. I just started." His voice was a rich timbre, made for radio or audio books.

"Nice to meet you. So, how'd you get here?" I inquired in a friendly tone.

"Do you know Grace? I was on a tour and she recruited me. I had a lot of interest in the house." He seemed self-assured and kind.

"Well, welcome. We need volunteers, so if you want to work weekends, let me know. Will chat later."

After that brief interlude, like many people at the Museum, including Grace who asked him to volunteer, I was captivated, even if it was only friendship. I met the devil and I'd soon have my first inkling of his modus operandi.

In a couple weeks, he'd volunteered during my weekend shifts, asked for my number, and wanted to hang out after hours. He'd text me first thing in the morning when I arrived at work, once or twice during the day, and the last thing at night before bed.

We'd entered what relationship experts call the fascination phase, where friendship or love is rosy, fun, and adventurous. But in reality, it was what crime and exploitation experts call targeting and grooming.

To be clear, I don't consider myself naïve. I'm in my late fifties. I've dated a lot, including a long term mature relationship that lasted longer than some marriages. I've worked in a variety of companies from indie ad agencies to large international corporations and have run my own art business since my teens. I've always worked more than one job, even if I had something full time I usually worked a side hustle of some sort. I was one of those people who watched mystery TV or movies and guessed the plot twist before most others.

But I'd also think, when watching true crime dramas, "that would never happen to me." Yet on several occasions, things did happen, and they weren't always pleasant. Andrew would become one of those things.

"Want to see a preview at Selkirk's?" His text lures me in. Selkirk's is everything a creative history buff could desire, art, antiques, and auctions.

"Oh yeah!" I eagerly text back.

"I received an exclusive invite. I'm looking at a bed frame. And we can grab lunch after."

"How about the London Tea Room?" I suggest.

"Perfect." And so began our first adventure a week later…

"Which bed did you want?" I asked Andrew as we perused Ivey Selkirk's preview of an upcoming auction. He spotted an auspicious bed frame in the online catalog. We perused a selection of high end art and antiques. He wore a pinstriped blue and white oxford shirt, a crème colored jacked, navy trousers and designer loafers. He dressed like he was meant to be shopping for a vintage bed worth at least ten thousand dollars. I wore a pinstriped shirt dress and black leggings. We appeared very Ladue and attracted the attention of no less than three of the staff that most likely saw a sale in their midst.

About twenty minutes before he'd picked me up at the Museum in his shiny black Mercedes. We spent another ten minutes trying to find a space to park. When he couldn't parallel park and I offered, began the moment I'd be driving him everywhere like I was his chauffeur. He walked briskly ahead of me towards the auction house, which was in a stunning historic building downtown. I was still recovering from a knee injury six months before and I waddled like an impregnated duck behind him, slightly embarrassed that I couldn't quite keep up.

I wanted to shoot footage for social media, so I asked for permission to film, paid much attention to the architecture and pieces in the showing, including an impressive silver plated drink service. We admired the paintings and wealthy accruements as he told me about his family. How his father died and left him a decent sum of money, but he needed to hold onto a job to fulfill the requirements of the trust. Andrew told me he was employed as a regional manager for a national drug store chain. I say reportedly because this would be the first of many things about Andrew that were questionable. It was also the beginning of epically long days out, because after an hour of endless questions about priceless pictures and the bed frame he sought, we hadn't even made it to lunch yet.

2 TEA TIME

"I will exalt my throne above the stars of God...I will be like the most High."
-Isiah 14: 14-15

"Don't stir your tea like that." Andrew scowled thru glossy black framed sunglasses with fogged lenses. Our tea arrived and he posed for selfies holding his cup wearing the shades.

I was taken aback by the criticism, gingerly pulling my teaspoon from my cup where it had squealed against the sides as I stirred. I flushed with a woeful ineptitude. I'd been a tea lover and was one of the bakers at the very tearoom where we were enjoying lunch. However, I hadn't practiced sophisticated table manners in a long time.

We sat at an expansive portrait window facing Locust Street inside the London Tea Room, three blocks away from the Museum. The summer sun shone brightly on the street outside.

"You press back and forth like this. My mother taught me. And don't dump your sugar in like that, you let it fall of the spoon." Andrew admonished. He sat like a king holding court, preparing for a feast. "I'm surprised you don't know this." He glibly goes on about how his family relocated to a high-end area of St. Louis when he was young. And so, begin the tales about how his mother went from being a divorced single mom of two to a remarried socialite in Ladue and his famous family connections.

Part of me feels like a five-year-old called to the front of the class for misbehaving, guilty despite working for the best tearoom in the city. But then again, as a savory baker I was more worried about how things tasted. I guess I thought of myself as the help and not a guest.

"Um, I didn't know that. I don't pretend to know everything." I pause as our traditional three-plate tier towers of food arrived. We ordered both afternoon and high teas full sweet and savory delights. We enjoyed Coronation salad on croissants (I made the salad in the kitchen a couple days before) and cucumber tea sandwiches with the crusts cut, scones, jam and clotted cream, Madeleines, a yummy mousse topped with berries and macarons.

"Our scones are amazing." I eagerly place one on my plate, cut it open using a knife, and begin lathering on the clotted cream.

"You don't cut your scone, you pull it apart, like this." With a gentle twist and flick of his wrist, his scone came apart easily.

God, some Ladue people, I cringe. Note, for non-St. Louisans, Ladue is a wealthy suburb of West St. Louis County. Coming from a low brow Catholic family of five, raised in the middle class area of South County, I'm not keen on snobbery.

"I have to ask the St. Louis question, where'd you go to high school?" I change the convo course to feed his ego while debating in my head if this is a friendship I want to cultivate.

"I graduated from Broughton, a boarding school up east because my father went there, like his father did. But I attended MICDS until my junior year. My father, although coming from money was self-made. He became a lawyer, then a judge in Chicago, retired and then became a stockbroker. My mother was divorced with two kids, my step-brother and sister. Her family owned a farm in north central Illinois. She was a server at a country club when he asked her out. And then I came along." He sips his tea with smug satisfaction. "What else do you do?"

I talk about my art and books, how I'd been trying to hone in on my niche, and was finding the most success on TikTok. "I've have ten thousand followers." I show him my page on my phone.

"I'll follow you." As Andrew grabs my phone, I see a man pull up, park and jump out to take pictures of the historic buildings across the street. I recognize him.

"Oh, there's Tony, he's a board member and volunteer from the Museum." I pipe up.

Andrew scrolls through my phone. "Mmm."

"He's a decent historian. Done a lot of research for the Museum." I watched Tony shoot several pictures and then he hopped into his car.

"What?"

"That guy, over there, across the street. You just missed him. He's a historian for the Museum."

Andrew glanced nonchalantly over his shoulder to peer out the window as Tony drove off. Looking back, I'll wonder if this was an odd omen for what was to come.

"I guess I'll have to meet him at some point." He hands me my phone and delves into the food. We have similar tastes in music and pop culture, and our paths came remarkably close to crossing previously at multiple places including Lemp Mansion.

"I am a Lemp descendent."

"What? Really."

"I mean, I don't tell everyone. There was kind of a controversy. My grandfather may have been illegitimate. But I have a lot of things from my family. And I lived in Milwaukee for a while near some of my Pabst relatives. I volunteered at the Pabst Mansion too. I love historic homes."

"I noticed you had Wisconsin plates. Have you been back long?" My curiosity was piqued.

"No, I got a transfer last autumn when my dad passed away."

“I’m so sorry. My father passed from complications with Covid a couple years ago. What happened? Or if you don’t want to talk about it, I understand.”

“No, it’s okay. He had a stroke and didn’t recover well. I came home to assist my mom.”

“That’s rough. My mom and older sister were both disabled from multiple sclerosis. It can be difficult.”

“They’re dead?”

“Yeah, but they both lived long lives with the disease although my mom’s was the remitting form. My sister’s was the progressive. That was harder, she was only twenty-three when she was diagnosed.”

“How about something more pleasant? You do pet portraits?”

“Yes.” I show him some of my best charcoal and pastel pieces from social media and photos on my phone.

“You should draw my dog. Well, the dog I used to have. I gave him up when I moved. And then he passed.” He shows me a picture of the cutest ball of white fluff as a notification pops up on his phone. “Oh, I have to go. We have to do this again soon.” He nods to our server for the check.

“Yeah, this was fun.” I wait patiently as he pulls out his wallet. I pause uncomfortably from etiquette confusion. I know he’s gay, but he’s also loaded and was the one who asked me to lunch. This was one of the few times that he actually paid for anything, although he gets to use my pretty generous employee discount. I wonder if he’s always this cheap acting for a wealthy person. I’ll find out later my gut is right.

3 A BED FIT FOR A KING

"For they cannot sleep unless they do evil; they are robbed of sleep unless they make someone stumble."

-Proverbs 4:16

"Ethan is over here on all fours on the floor in my apartment." Andrew texts and I smirk to myself. He's always chasing someone. I hate to break it to him, but my friend that was in the process of installing his mattress wasn't the least the bit interested. I'd find out much later that my acquaintance had been suspicious of Andrew from their initial meeting.

Several weeks earlier…

"Listen, Ethan owns his own mattress shop. I'm sure he could find something for you. You just need to pick out a frame." I am frustrated, worn down from searching for bed frames in multiple places. When Andrew told me he'd been sleeping on his couch or an air mattress since he'd relocated, we were on a mission to get a bed for him. We've hit everywhere from outlet and thrift stores to massive antique malls. We are having another epic picking and shopping day and have paused to get lunch at Square One Brewery in Lafayette Square. "I thought you were using the frame from your family's farm?"

"I'm not so sure," Andrew squints as he plays on my phone. We are scrolling through dozens of listings on Facebook marketplace and other places online. Over the last couple of months, since we were at Selkirk's, I've made at least five serious inquiries of bed frames. It's a pain in the ass, messaging back various sellers around the St. Louis area.

I'm doing most of this work because his phone sucks, and he can't have a Facebook account for some stupid reason. And he still has his crap phone. Why he couldn't get past his old iPhone ten, I'll never understand. I'm finding this stinginess weird. A revelation about his social media accounts and scrolling habits will shock me in the future.

But here in the present, he slaps my phone on the table in frustration.

"Hey, don't do that." I protest and grab it back. I bought my iPhone 13 ProMax with two terabytes of memory specifically for the camera, photography and the ability to share my art on social media and online. It was an investment I planned to keep it for a long while. I wasn't letting him abuse my phone.

"Sorry," he grumbled and picked up his phone to check dating apps as the waitress came by to take our order. We decide on chicken strips and loaded kettle potato chips.

"Did you want the frame at Selkirk's?"

"No. Once I saw it in person, I didn't like it." He snorts and continues to flip through dating profiles.

He found a bed frame in Alton that showed a lot of promise and the price is amazing. But Andrew bemoaned that the center piece of the foot board is warped from water damage. The seller is now throwing in a wardrobe. "I can attempt to salvage it. I'd have to cut out the damaged panel, but then you could replace it with some cool fabric," I offer.

"I dunno." He gripes.

I will begin to hate when he's like this, moody and undecided. It will happen more often by autumn. "Plus, now she's throwing in an armoire." I show him the latest message from the seller.

"I want to keep searching," he snorts disappointingly. Our food arrives and he wolfs it down like he's never had loaded potato chips. *So much for the elegant table manners of the upper crust*, I muse to myself.

"Well, you know you need a mattress," I remind him. "Let's set an appointment with Ethan."

Andrew caves, he sets a date and brings the headboard that supposedly belonged to a family ancestor from the farm to Ethan's shop.

The visit was strange. I made introductions and after a quick peek at Ethan's new motorcycle, and removing the headboard from Andrew's car, we step inside try out the mattresses. Andrew sits and lays down on several. I can tell he's ambivalent. Ethan educates him on what to look for in a decent mattress. I can tell Andrew is bored but satisfied. Ethan talks in depth about the bed frame and getting side boards and brackets that will work, writes up the ticket, and explains the cost.

"Oh, that's a lot." Andrew didn't seem to listen to most of what Ethan said, put in his earbuds, and claimed he should contact his mother on what to spend. "It seems kind of expensive." He stepped out for a moment to make a call.

I'm weirdly uncomfortable. I've worked a lot of retail, high end and average joe shops. I've sold customers a variety of things, from junior sized teen clothing to men's accessories, to vintage and antiques. Andrew's disinterest in something he needs is troubling, especially if he has the funds.

"Okay, let's do it." Andrew returns, tugs his card out of his wallet and then scrolls through his phone as the transaction goes through.

"I'll call when it's ready and we'll work out the delivery," Ethan assures him, hands him the receipt, and we walk out to the car. "Thanks, have a good one."

"Now it's done. You'll at least have something. You can always put it aside once you get what you want," I assured as we drove off.

"Did you think that was too much?" Andrew wavered. "My mom thought it was a bit expensive."

I grimace and cringe inwardly. *What forty-year-old calls his mother for approval to buy a bed?*

"He's giving you a great bed, it's the mattress and box spring," I protest mildly. His indecision is annoying.

"Well..."

"You say your back is bothering you. And you're not sleeping well."

"Some of that is work. I have to also get permission for expenses from mother."

"Okay, but this is a need and not a want. Let's get lunch." I'm done arguing. He can't make a decision for shit.

"You're buying."

"Fine. We'll celebrate the bed." I cheer him on.

"The bed is coming. Can you help me?" Andrew texts two days after our adventure at the shop.

"Sure." I agree.

A week later, we do the first organization of his apartment to prepare for the incoming bed. Andrew's apartment is like his own personal house museum, decorative antiques, figurines and pieces everywhere. We move some of his bedroom furniture and paintings to create room for his impending heavenly slumber. We also cleaned out some silver he didn't need as we warmed up snacks.

"What do you think of these? My grandmother's." He shows me a stunning cutlery set that's missing pieces.

"Oh, pretty." I have a thing for silverware and admire the glistening arrangement nestled in a burgundy velvet lined box.

"We should have tea sometime and use them."

"Yes, we should."

In the midst of finishing the cleaning and after our snack, Andrew facetimes a guy he's hung up on. They've been out a couple of times after meeting on an app. Most recently they went to an auction and the new guy, I'll call Bill, bought some Rothko-Esque pop art. They are chatting briefly before Andrew swings the phone my way.

"Hey! Let me introduce you to Victoria."

"Hi!" I wave. Bill is kinda of cute, absolutely more gay. I feel bad for the guy because it's a totally random call. The prospective keeper boyfriend has that deer in the headlights look when Andrew pops on the camera.

"We're making room for my new bed." Andrew is flush with excitement.

"Nice. You want to see where I put the paintings? And I have to show you how I hand painted my refrigerator." Billy enthuses.

We're given a mini tour as Billy bounces around his apartment which is completely different eclectic mix of eras. The gold and black zebra striped fridge is a definite nod to eighties excess. I confess, I'm bored at this point and getting tired. I came over right after work and am ready for a shower. They hang up after blowing kisses. Bill is nice, but I have a feeling he's not enough in a multitude of ways for Andrew.

"You like him?"

"There's something about him. Bill bought two fantastic pieces of art, but the rest of his apartment? Everything clashes. He has no taste or sense of style. Did I tell you he lives in High Ridge with a couple of lesbians? And they have cats," he whines.

I raise a brow as I listen to him debate the budding relationship out loud. It's moments like these when he's so uppity, it drives me nuts. "You giving it a chance or not?"

"I don't know." He fusses for another five minutes before we finish eating and wrap up our bed prep project.

A month later, Andrew has bought a completely different frame from anything we'd searched for. Put together, the bed is magnificent, the foot board has curved edges and is painted with Greco roman details. He forgot he owned a theme matching burgundy and gold bedspread and curtains in storage. It's magnificent when put together.

"I've already had a three way on it." he effuses.

"Damn, how did you find the room on a queen size?" is all I can muster.

4 ON THE HUNT

"The curse of the Lord is in the house of the wicked: but he blesseth the habitation of the just."

-Proverbs 3:33

"You want to check out a house?" The text comes over and I am instantly flattered to be invited. I'm even more impressed when he sends the link and it's a gorgeous Italianate Victorian in Lafayette Square, located southwest of downtown St. Louis. I am surprised that he wants to go considering that earlier that morning he sent me a pic of him sitting in a hot salt bath to calm his hemorrhoids.

Lafayette is a stunning, higher-end neighborhood, full of mostly rehabbed historic homes that border Lafayette Park, the oldest Victorian park west of the Mississippi. It is absolutely one of my favorite places on the planet. I've used the area as a main location for most of my steampunk novels.

Days later, we're driving around the Lafayette neighborhoods on a hot summer day before the house viewing. I give Andrew a mini tour, showing where my great-grandmother's house used to be where the Walgreen's now stands on the segment known as Bohemian Hill. We do a quick lap around the park. My paternal grandparents were married and my father baptized in St. Joseph's chapel which was rehabbed to be a residence four years ago. It's on the north side of the park which is filled with a wide variety of people enjoying the day.

It's soon time for us to see the house. It's one of a particular row of what was four attached houses on Kennett. The one farthest east was unfortunately damaged in the historic 1896 tornado, leaving three behind.

We meet the realtor out front. I am immediately transported the minute we walk up the stone steps. The house is stunning, utilizing the original flooring, baseboards and trim. The dark woodwork contrasts nicely against the white walls. The fireplaces are grand with carved marble and embossed cover plates. I adored that the owners kept the Victorian aesthetics but modernized the necessary elements like the kitchen appliances.

"Holy crap," I whisper as we walk into the parlor bordered by the original pocket doors. I nearly squeal when I notice they have the original keyhole plates.

Andrew raves as the realtor walks us through until we get to the bathroom. It has a floor-to-ceiling window.

"That's odd." He smirks. "Why would someone do that?"

"I bet that's where it connected to the neighboring house." A quick aside, later I'd find that I was correct in this assumption. "You could cover it using curtains or stained glass overlay."

Andrew groaned. He has a right to be picky. We stroll into the dining room which has a low hanging impressive art deco brass chandelier that was rescued from a hotel that burned down.

We trot up a fancy staircase. He's disappointed that there's no master bath. But the bedrooms are immense.

"Would you move in with me?" He asks while checking out yet another fireplace.

"Well, um yeah." I freeze. I have lived alone since I was thirty. That's over twenty-five years of having my own space. Freedom. I haven't committed to much other than my art and books because my word is my bond. I show up. I follow through. I execute. I can easily remember the times I backed out of events, because it's so few in number.

I once showed up to a photo shoot I was costuming with a hundred degree fever. I did another shoot the day after my sister died, and later that week I had a book signing and another shoot. I used to be one of those people that would be near death and still show up for work. Note, especially since Covid and because I value myself more, I no longer do this. However, I do my best to keep my promises.

"I'd love to, but we'd have to talk about it. When you planning on moving?"

"My lease isn't up until May, I can afford to break it. But I'm not sure I want to."

"Well, I'm leaving the Museum in March next year. I'll need a place by then." I've already been looking way in advance. This could be a better option, but I'm honest from the get-go. "I'd have to know how much rent you'd charge, because honestly, I can't afford this neighborhood."

"I like this, what do you think?"

"I fucking love it."

"You'd need your own bath though, or I would. That bathroom deserves another upgrade. It'd be an additional thirty thousand." We head to the basement. It's completely refinished and mold free. There's another sink, fridge and microwave for entertaining. Plenty of room for additional living space and storage. We return to the kitchen.

"I'm not impressed with this sink." Andrew grumbles. It's in the island in the middle of the room set in a speckled blue and white granite. It's large and deep, resplendent a modern faucet that has a lot of water pressure, and an angled bottom for better drainage. For someone that doesn't even use a dishwasher, I don't believe that Andrew is a proper judge of the sink. A new microwave is in a stationed pantry. The oven is immense but kind of crammed into the corner. A storage drawer contains paper history on the house. "But you could bake a lot of scones in here. We could throw some awesome parties." He grins.

The realtor leads us out and down wooden stairs into the yard which is enclosed by tall wooden privacy fencing. We walk the inlaid brick to the side area. It's large enough to hold a small gazebo. There are several impressive flower beds and shrubbery lining the house and barely any grass to cut. Other than a couple of unexpected mosquito bites, the garden was adorable.

"It has a two-car garage." The realtor leads us in and notes that the door was new. I notice it has one of the better entries for a garage as it's right where the street and alley meets, allowing for easy entry.

"We'd both have enough room to park and for storage." Andrew scans the space.

"What do you think?" The realtor smiles.

"I like it, but I'll do research on the bathrooms."

"Well, let me know." She walks us out.

Once we're in the car? "Oh my God, I love it. But I'd totally talk them down. I'm not in a rush. What did you think?"

"It's gorgeous. The woodwork on the main floor is in excellent condition."

"And that chandelier! Imagine eating underneath that."

For a moment I'm caught up in the grandeur, the beauty of this Victorian stunner. It won't last.

"I need to see another house." Andrew texts. We're off to see one in Richmond Heights that's a waste of time.

"Look at that turret!" he exclaims as we pull up, but the excitement dies.

The area is decent, but they're asking an inflated price. In the walkthrough Andrew extends his arms in the kitchen and can almost touch the walls on either side. I don't even bother to head upstairs to see the bedrooms. He's totally disinterested. There's no witty banter, no compliments. We chat on the driveway with the realtor, Andrew talks about having to move his mother, but soon the humidity overwhelms us and we hop into the Mercedes.

On the drive out Andrew remarks, "Did you hear that? I asked her if she was interested in selling my mother's house in Ladue. She doesn't put up homes for sale. What is that about?"

"Strange."

"I've got to hire a better upscale realtor." He snorts.

Now I'll always wonder if she had an inkling he wasn't legitimately interested. He was using these viewings to boost his ego. Later I'd find it was worse than that.

We head over to the Fountain on Locust for lunch afterwards where he continues to gripe.

"I still can't believe she wouldn't list my mother's house."

"You'll find someone else. Maybe it's not a good match." I offer.

We order salads that they can convert into wraps and kettle chips. Everything is delicious. He eats in mere seconds. No wonder he has digestion issues. Our moment of contentment is broken as he realizes he needs to pay his rent.

"My card won't work for rent." Andrew pecks at the phone, trying multiple times to get the payment to go through.

"Let me help." I notice right off that he has a million apps open and he's having trouble getting a signal. His phone is beat up. "Close out all these apps."

"It should still work," he grumbles and swipes furiously on his busted technological dinosaur.

"Okay, you're not getting air." I tether his phone Wi-Fi to mine. It works better. "See? Let's try it again." But not surprisingly, it still has issues. "I'll pay for lunch if you have bank problems."

"That's not it. I have to fix this!" Andrew loses it, breaks out in a sweat, and runs outside for close to ten minutes. He finally returns, still white as a sheet. "The bank thinks it's the rent app. I'll have to call my landlord tomorrow."

We split lunch, and as I exit, I realize I'm agitated, having taken on his stress and need a nap.

A couple weeks later, Andrew volunteers on a weekend I'm working.

"I had no idea you lived in the Museum."

"Oh, yeah. I've been the caretaker for over five years. This sixth one is my last. I've been here longer than anyone else in this position. Also, the oldest. I like it, but it's time to give someone else a chance. I move out in March of next year." He apparently forgot I told him this before.

Andrew wielded this fact to his advantage. Texting that he finished work or a tryst nearby and "did I want to go for a drive" or to come by and explore the museum. At first I thought he was lonely and needed a friend. But he had multiple bang outs with guys in the lofts in the neighborhood or at the sauna in downtown west so he was always conveniently close by even though he lived way the heck out in St. Charles County.

As time passed, Andrew forgot that I was moving. I wasn't sure if it was his disinterest, his hearing loss (if that was even true) or if he was hyper focused on something else. There were moments when we were driving that he was consistently scrolling, often burning through the battery on his beat up phone two to three times per trip. It was always on the charger in his car.

"Let's run over to Ladue and I'll show you my mom's house." Andrew grinned as he arrived on another evening out.

"Sounds awesome." I'm genuinely excited to see where he grew up.

"I'll show you that donor's house that's preparing to be demolished." One of the multitude of places Andrew volunteered for was gifted a house from an estate. The institution was offered its contents which they sold. The house had been on the market for some time but was purchased for the land value. "Apparently it'd been vacated a long while and they said it had mold." There wasn't much to see and we left. "Let's see my mom's."

It was after eight and the sun was long down when we pulled into the oldest neighborhood in Ladue.

"Doesn't it seem like the house where the kid was left behind at Christmas?"

"Yeah." And indeed, it does. It's a two-story brick mansion, a circle drive and two expensive cars parked in front.

"It's too much for mother to upkeep. We have to sell it soon." He mused aloud, "let's pop over to the next neighborhood. I want to show you something else."

I drive over to the next street. "These are still some of the oldest subdivisions in Ladue." He beams. "That house? That's where my ex Curt and I lived. It was his grandparents' house and they gave it to us as a wedding gift." Curt was the great-grandson of the Lambert Field family, supposedly. Andrew showed me Curt's picture on his phone, an incredibly handsome man, a swath of brown hair bordered by grey accents, chocolate brown eyes, a strong jawline, and a natural tan. He stood in front of a light colored brick building with black awnings.

"He's hot."

We move on to look at other homes in the area before Andrew realizes he has to get to bed early.

After the truth came out, I searched for Curt's information everywhere. His picture didn't exist as far as I researched, the Lambert family didn't have any descendants of his name, and certainly none of them were gay and married to Andrew. Andrew had never been married.

The house in Lafayette was listed for over eight hundred thousand, was reduced somewhat and sold in about twelve weeks to my dismay. Another house in that trio would be up for sale three months later and sold before they held the open house for us to see it.

Andrew claimed to have a "budget" of around seven hundred fifty thousand, but I'd find out that this was a lie as well. I will always wonder if the first agent seemed disinterested because she'd caught onto his game.

We passed by and walked through some of the most storied neighborhoods and homes in the St. Louis area. We continued to search for houses accompanied by two different realtors deep into the fall. The ones that were for sale and we viewed in person? He had no real intention of buying. He never purchased or put in any real bids on any of the houses we looked at.

5 HITTING THE BINS & THE BRICKS

"Whoever seeks good finds favor but evil comes to one who searches for it."
-Proverbs 11:27

"Fuck Kingside Diner." Andrew texts. I can almost see the grimace on his face. We are debating where to eat after we cruised around. We are both reminded of a food poisoning experience at the local eatery.

"Have you ever been to the bins?" The intro of this convo was nicer.

"The Goodwill outlet? Oh yeah." I feel the rush of an impressive find impending.

This will be the first of our prolific adventurous excursions to thrift and resale shops. We hit up the Goodwill Outlet warehouse off of Market Street. For the uninitiated, this is a massive building, where the remaining pickings of the regional Goodwill stores go. You should bring work or gardening gloves because some of the items get manhandled, broken and dirty. A second outlet store was later added near the airport. It's busy, fun, crazy, sometimes disappointing, sometimes incredible. We once did both outlets in a day. I was exhausted but found a couple fun things.

That first adventure was on a Sunday. The main location doesn't open until 3 p.m. and eager pickers were lined up along the entry ramp beforehand. The parking lot was packed. It's like the running of the bulls as the doors open. If you don't hurry and get a cart first thing, the rest of your trip will be hell as you're hauling your discoveries around the store wishing you'd grow an extra pair of arms to hold it all. They charge by the weight for most of the items. They roll out massive bins that are about four foot wide, six feet long and a foot deep. Some people wait at the swinging doors for new bins to be pushed out for the public. This is the gold rush of thrift stores.

I find a ton of awesome textiles for steampunk stuff. In the past I've found a mini desk, china, DVD's and collectibles. My best find by far was an authentic men's naval military pea coat that was left on a bin of books during my first ever visit. I poked around, snatched it up and examined it. No smells, tears and the original serviceman's tag was still inside. It also had the rare brass buttons that were only used for about ten years. I know this because of one of my relatives served in the Navy. It cost me a grand total of $1.75. I later resold it on Etsy for $125.

We are soon buried in piles of rejected merchandise from other stores, hoping for the rare find of a designer bag, clothing, or a handy practical item like tools or shoes. We bemoan a whole stack of poster prints that are damaged from people not realizing their value. It's also a fantastic place to find picture frames. "This is gorgeous." He snags a gilded gold piece perfect for his antique décor.

On another visit Andrew hit the jackpot. "Look at this bin." He is grinning wildly as he pulls out pair after pair of extra-large designer socks. We match a bunch of others. One pair is still in the original package displaying a Neiman Marcus tag. "This is a $40 pair of socks."

"Wow. Someone with extraordinary taste."

Another visit led to four bins full of stunning coffee table books. I tugged out an impressive impressionistic one and handed it to him. "Take this, it's worth $125."

"I dunno." Andrew's ADHD is on fire as he sorts through the massive mound of books. We made way for two couples that have already collected a mother lode from the same batch and are heading for check out. He opens the art book and flips through to the back dust jacket. "How did you know the price?" He gazes at me incredulously.

"I'm an author and have my art degree, remember?" I laugh. I have a good eye. I end up taking only two books, on fashion history and textiles. Andrew has a pile of at least ten.

On the opposite end of the bins in the St. Louis market are the thrift and resale shops of West County, one of which is St. Vincent's on Olive.

"You ready bitch?" Andrew smirked as we pulled up.

"Oh yeah!" I have been here before too and found an amazing lamp for small art shows and some high-end scarves and purses.

We sort through figurines and housewares first. I'm not finding anything I have to have. But the clothing is another, more pleasant matter.

"Oh my God." Andrew discovers a cache of designer dress shirts in his size. He debates over the bins and still ends up holding about ten shirts and sweaters. I find three boat neck three-quarter sleeve length shirts from Talbot's. We've come on a sale day. I spend a whopping $11. I am ecstatic later that evening when I try them on.

"Come look at this." Andrew urges and I follow him to a locked case at the checkout. Inside is a stunning gilded historical framed fan marked at $125.

"Wow, that is something."

"I can't decide." He debates and we leave it in the case. Eventually he changes his mind and it ends up in his apartment after he makes a return visit for it.

After that first adventure at the Outlet, we decide to nosh at Kingside Diner in the CWE. I've eaten there on several visits including on the patio and during the Halloween in the Central West End Halloween party.

It's after the lunch hour rush and it seems to take a while for us to get seated. We both decide to get their Caprise grilled cheese sandwiches with the extra offered chicken and cokes. The restaurant isn't full and guests leave as we order, yet it still seems too long to get served. Working in food service, I'm trying to be patient. Andrew is chomping at the bit, displaying his usual impatience, checking his phone and people watching as we sit at the window.

The sandwiches finally arrive. Andrew hates his, chows down his fries and ends up eating some of my fries too. “Something is wrong with this chicken.”

And there is. It’s hard on the outside and rubbery on the inside. As I made chicken salad for the Tea Room, baking forty to eight pounds of chicken a week, I can tell it’s been precooked, refrigerated or frozen and reheated. The outside of the breast is hardened and the inside is watery. It completely ruined the cheesy goodness of the sandwich. I pack my other half to go. We get a chocolate shake and share it.

“This is too expensive.” He groans at the check. “Twelve for a crappy sandwich and two for bad chicken.” We can’t get a hold of the server to complain. His legendary restlessness is flaring. We don’t spend much longer inside and head out.

Later that day I get up from a nap and see a text. “I’m not feeling well.” *Oh no.* He’s dealt with disordered eating and physical digestive issues for a long time. I don’t think much of it otherwise.

Next morning, he messages, “I’m so sick.” I had a bad episode of gas in the middle of the night, so I throw out my other half of the sandwich as a precaution. I email the contact for the restaurant rather than leaving a bad review but never hear anything back. It becomes a thing that every time we eat out, he jokes about “fucking Kingside Diner.”

“I am not well.” Andrew texts.

“Oh no, what?” I reply.

I’m at my job at the city on a Tuesday shortly after the Kingside incident and I’m preparing to wrap up for the day. I’m getting ready to text when Andrew calls right after I text. He sounds absolutely desolate.

“Billy dumped me.”

“But you didn’t really like him, right? Are you okay?”

“I’m having a breakdown.”

"We could do something after I get off work."

"I dunno."

"Let's go to the movies, we never did see the tornado movie." I suggest. I commence scrolling through movie times on the local theatre app. "Catch the rush hour deal."

"Um, okay. I'm gonna leave here shortly." He lived way out in St. Charles County, northwest of St. Louis. I suggest we meet at the theatre. I just have to select purchase on the movie app and we're set.

The moment I'm off work, I'm trotting the three city blocks to the Museum. At one point I trip over a raised sidewalk and nearly fall in a hurry to help him. All I can think is that he's suicidal and really needs to talk. By the time I drop off my work stuff and freshen up my makeup, Andrew is close by. He pulls up and I plop in the driver's seat.

"I don't want to do a movie. Let's hit a bar or something." He sounds flattened.

"Okay." I'm disappointed, but I bend to him because he's apparently wounded. This would be the first of a multitude of emotional collapses Andrew had, a minor one in comparison to some of the others that followed. "Where we going?"

"I dunno, just drive." He grumbles. His bipolar/ADHD makes his indecision and focus worse.

For a creative person, I'm pretty well on track with what has to be done. I journal and set my plans each day. I'm wise enough to know that I'm toast without my calendar planner. This difference in our personalities later helped me recover from his insane clutches of attention and desperation. I click off the pending ticket purchase movie app and we roll.

"Let's go to the bar at the Chase." He slowly decides.

Parking is kind of a nightmare, considering it's happy hour/dinner time, but we manage to find a spot in a garage nearby. As he eagerly strides ahead of me, I'm reminded that I need to be in better shape before I move next year.

“Are we getting a table?” The dining area is filling up quickly. It’s been an exceptionally long while since I’d been in this space and it’s been completely upgraded.

“Um, let’s sit at the bar.”

For the next ninety minutes he drowns his sorrows in martinis and mixed drinks. The convo runs from how his father used to come to this place, to the hot married men obviously in town for a convention, to his past lovers he nailed at this hotel, and how he loves a hot actor on a devil show. “I could be Lucifer,” he boasts as he swills his martini.

I’m not in the mood for alcohol and decide to order food for us to share. He claims he’s not hungry, but of course he sponges off my plate. Note, to the casual reader, the following may come across as catty or uncaring. But in truth, this is how Andrew operated, using his catastrophic needs for sympathy, favors and attention. His scrounging annoys me, not because I don’t want to share, or for money issues, but because for someone that reportedly has a load of wealth, he’s pretty freaking cheap and the more wasted he gets, the sloppier he acts. Plus, he thought Billy was an uneducated hick.

Andrew’s sweater comes off, he unbuttons his collar. He scrolls the dating apps in between bemoaning Billy and ordering additional alcohol. He is in a spiral of manic and depressed moods collapsing on each other in a dizzying fall.

I listen and listen, being kind, being a good friend. He leaves for the bathroom. I noticed that the bartender had been watching him the whole afternoon and I got his number for Andrew. I’ve been an effective wing woman for my gay friends. But this wouldn’t matter because after we leave the bar, we drive past several grand houses nearby and through Forest Park. I’m fairly certain that after he drops me off, he has a rebound hook up planned at the sauna.

Months later, I realize, like many plans we made, we never did see Twisters.

6 STORMING THE BASTILLE

"Do not repay anyone evil for evil. Be careful to do what is right in the eyes of everyone."
-Romans 12:17

"Hurry up, we gotta go." Andrew, although drunk, is moving quickly over the brick laid sidewalks of Soulard on the way back to his car. I swear I will never be able to catch up.

"Okay, okay. You found a hook up. Let me stop and get a cookie."

"I don't have time."

About two hours earlier…

"What are you doing?" Andrew texts as I am working on a book and craving sweets. I am kicking myself for not getting something to chew on at the grocery store earlier in the week. It's after eight and everything close and safe downtown is closed.

"I was thinking of getting a snack…" I pause typing. I know that he has an itch that needs to be scratched, but I bite, "okay, ETA?"

I try not to judge, I've always believed that what goes on in people's bedrooms are their business. I know of a single week there was possibly fifteen to twenty guys Andrew was with. And he doesn't want to be alone. He desires to be in a relationship but is also seriously horny.

His parade of claimed lovers included a wealthy attorney, a popular local TV weatherman (in a hotel at Union Station), multiple police officers including one that was getting married to a woman in only six weeks, the heir to a furniture store fortune (reportedly in a car outside of Brio in Frontenac Plaza), and a high end realtor. He was just as fascinated by discussing his sordid trysts at the gym with glory holes and multiple partners in the sauna. Why he chose to confide in me, I'll never know. I wish I hadn't heard any of it. It was probably just boasting anyway.

"I suppose I shouldn't go. It'd be bad if I got caught. Mother would be disappointed." I wonder if he wanted to get caught so it'd force him to stop his erratic behavior. He said he desired to be in a real relationship and yet he rejected some nice guys, including a charming husky opera singer.

He picked me up at the Museum, and we sped around until we ended up in Soulard, and are soon seeking parking, led by his repetitive indecisiveness.

"Oh, let's stop here. Insomnia Cookies!" I exclaim as we drive by.

"Do they have alcohol?"

"No..."

"Well, you don't need it, we're not stopping. I need a drink. Oh hey..."

We settle on the Bastille. I've been there once before, as a safe space to get a drink and hit the bathroom during Mardi Gras long ago.

We stumble into a quirky vibe. It's a pleasant, well decorated dive bar, filled with a wide variety of affable gay men. I am mostly likely the only female born patron, a fruit fly along for the ride. I've done this plenty of times before in the 1990's but my close gay friends left St. Louis by the early 2000's. It's funny how the wafts of cologne, beverages, and cigarette smoke hasn't changed in over twenty years.

I'm wearing a nice sweater and leggings. Andrew is of course dressed like a 1980's stockbroker. We seem like a Ladue couple seeking to swing on a Saturday night.

"My stepbrother is supposed to live close to here. He won't talk to me." He saunters to the bar as I sit on yet another bar stool. For once he pays for drinks. I'm trying to hold onto cash for ice cream afterwards.

At the onset, Andrew picks apart most of the other patrons using catty, condescending remarks. While it's true that he's probably the most attractive man in the bar, I find this dragging behavior boring.

He talks about Cory, a guy he met in Illinois. Cory was an airline pilot married to an attractive woman. He shows me a picture of them together. They are a stunning couple, even in casual clothes. "I had an affair with him. He was my first guy after Curt. I loved him so much, I wanted to get married. So, he says he can't do it anymore, and he goes back to his wife. Well, a couple months later? He leaves his wife for another dude. I was devastated."

He pauses then opens up about Curt, his ex-husband.

"He was an amazing man, older than me. We met at a Ladue Club party, he was twenty-one and I was sixteen, his family knew mine. I wasn't driving yet and wanted to leave. Of course I wasn't out yet, but he offered to drive me home. I had the wildest crush on him. When we pulled up, he put his hand on my thigh and told me I could talk to him about anything. He returned to school, then law school and came back. I went onto Broughton and then Brown. I started seeing guys, but Curt was my real first. We dated off and on forever." Andrew pauses for moment, caught up in the memories, then continues. "We went to a real Carnival ball in Venice! It began with a ride in the canals to a legit castle. It was something out of a movie. We were dressed to the nines, masks, costumes! It was completely lantern and candle lit. We had sex on a balcony outside."

"Oh wow." I'm impressed. "How cool is that."

The more Andrew drinks, the more the stories come. In between he does his phone scrolling. The bar fills up around us. The men around us are kind, but not one of them is his type. If he decides to go home with someone or have a fling, it won't be with someone from here. Although that might be what he needs is a person that's for real, not some pick up off of Grindr.

"We had a birthday picnic in Paris under the Eiffel Tower during my studies at the Beaux-Arts school." He blathers on about Curt. "We married in

Colorado where it was legal. But then he had an affair with another attorney in his office. I was crushed. With the family monies at stake it took years for the divorce to get finalized." He looks absolutely heartbroken in the dim shadows of the bar. I am astounded at the amount of experiences he's had.

"I'm so sorry." I genuinely am. He's obviously still not over it.

"We had the coolest house. Did I tell you our house was broken into?"

"Really?"

"We came home early from a barbecue at a neighbors and went to sleep early. About three am he hears this noise and wakes me. We call the police and nothing. A couple weeks later we're out of town and we get a call from his mother that the house was broken into. They stole some stuff but nothing earth shattering."

"Oh shit. That had to be scary." I'm shocked.

"You know the Ladue police were canvassing the neighborhood afterwards. Apparently a few other houses in the area got hit."

"I would think so."

"You know, you could make me a character in your books," he muses aloud and snaps a selfie.

"I might."

"I know, Lord Ladue. A vampire in West County. He sucks the blood of his enemies, preys on the wealthy. Heyyyyyy."

I can't help it, I cackle aloud. The group next to us glanced over.

"Hey." One of them chimes in then apologizes. "You look like you're having fun."

"Not with you," Andrew mumbles under his breath.

"He's being nice. Stop it." I can't fathom how rude he's being. We're in Soulard, not the Four Seasons.

"I'm Lord Ladue you know. I'm better than them." He continues to sip. "You know I told my mom that we get snacks from QuikTrip. She's all, 'Andrew, this woman has you eating gas station food, what is wrong with her?' I have to tell her the pizza is good though. We should've gotten a pizza instead."

Despite the alcohol, my craving for sweets has not stopped. I didn't feel like drinking my sugar that evening. The music volume and the voices are higher.

A chunky guy behind Andrew suddenly farted loudly. We are snickering. It is undoubtedly the funniest part of the evening.

After five or so drinks and a pithy attempt to have fun, Andrew's ready to leave. He nearly sprints to the car while I shuffle behind, still needing a cookie fix.

"Come on, hurry."

I hobble to the car and jump in.

"I have places to be." He's found his hook up and his anxiety is off the charts for someone that just drank a ton of alcohol.

"Alright, calm down."

Once at the Museum, I hurry out and he drives off in a flash. I'm too tired to head out for sweets and make a decaf tea.

I decide that I'm done with him and hanging out in bars after he leaves for his booty call. I'm feeling like a cross between a sober companion and a chauffeur. That night at the Bastille, I didn't get ice cream or cookies afterwards. I have to break this pattern.

7 SUNDAY DRIVES & INTIMATE CONVERSATIONS

"You have set out our iniquities before you, our secret sins in the light of your presence."
-Psalm 90:8

"You collect people." There's a hint of biting jealousy in Andrew's voice.

"Of course I do. I have networking talents, it's great part of the business, and I genuinely like people," I briefly blather. I don't apologize for having a lot of connections. It makes me a crafty creative businessperson. I sincerely love to see what others are creating. It took a lot of growth not to be jealous of what others had or what they were doing. I was a shy kid. I was easily influenced. I've come a long, long way.

It's hard to not be intimidated by his lineage. His list of claimed relatives included the Lemp and Pabst families, the Niedringhaus Foundry family and founders of Granite City, Illinois, Petring Coffee, the Donohue's of Woolworth's, Pullman Train Cars and Jane Oaker, a theatre and early screen actress.

We sit at Square One Brewery, which has come a tradition of ours on Sunday drives. I ran into the owner, said hello and updated her on a photo book on which I've been working. I shot pictures of the Cassilly sculpture fountain and a Steampunked model in their courtyard about a year before. That project was temporarily tabled after I knew I'd be moving.

I wonder why Andrew's acting this way, especially with his family's history and money. *Why suddenly so bitter?* I don't remember how the topic of the conversation changed, but I'm certain that we were at the point of our meal where I sent him pics of that day's adventures. It was like many Sundays where we puttered around like an elderly couple after church.

"Oh my GOD, what is that?" Andrew exclaimed in astonishment.

We turned onto a side street of the seedy industrial section of North Broadway. At the end of the street, in the bright late summer sunshine, a slender young woman sporting a bright pink bob hair cut in a hot pink bikini and brown leather vest stood and splashed herself in a bright blue kiddie pool with sparkling clean water (especially considering the area we were in). We simultaneously burst into laughter.

"This is so St. Louis," I cackled.

Earlier that afternoon we decided that today's mission was to find out where the Niedringhaus Foundry was. Andrew was a descendent of that family as well. He'd dug up an address that was a hair north of downtown St. Louis. We passed where Shady Jack's closed only a few months before. That warehouse building had been purchased and was supposed to become some sort of arts or entertainment complex.

When we arrived at the former address of the foundry and found an empty lot, I eased down the cross street to find our aforementioned punk beauty in the industrial desert. Our lady in pink simply glared at us as we passed.

I am laughing so hard that I'm close to hyperventilation.

"What in the hell?" Andrew twangs like country folk.

As we pulled into the parking lot behind the former Shady Jack's building, an older couple in a Beemer followed us into the lot. I drove along, looking at the addresses behind the building to see if any of the doors were in use. A couple random cars were parked near an entrance that seemed rehabilitated.

"You're going to get us killed. What is this?" Andrew moaned as we passed over rocky, bumpy barely-there road. "Aren't you scared?"

I giggle my response. “We’re fine.” But to answer his question, no, I wasn’t. “At this point I’ve heard six people shot and killed between 2011 and 2023, and I was shot at while the Museum was set on fire during the Floyd riots in 2020. Driving through this is nothing.” I laugh maniacally.

“You better not damage my car,” Andrew whines, having a full out panic attack.

“Chill, we’re turning around.” I circle around and the other luxury car tails us out to Broadway. As we stop at a light, another young lady in a bad dark wig, short shorts, a vest, and cowboy boots crosses in front of us. “Maybe they’re having a pool party.” We burst into laughter again. Although the building hunt was a bust, the drive had been fun.

“You know I have to ask where you went to high school.” I laugh at the popular St. Louis question as we drive through the Central West End on similar jaunt. We’re searching for yet another home that his family owned at one point. It’s a Niedringhaus home along Lindell. This family member owned an enameling and stamping company.

“Well, I went to MICDS for a couple years, but then my father sent me to Broughton up east.”

“Oh.” At this point I’m not sure how to respond to his displays of wealth other than be genuinely surprised at how the other half lives.

“Stop, there it is!” he exclaimed.

The house we were searching for is an all-out stone mansion including a massive turret on the corner. It’s now Ladue Nails, a salon business.

“We need to set an appointment!” We come around to get a better look and pull over to check the details. They are open on Sundays, but they’ve already closed by the moment we drive past. We read through the historical details on his phone. Unlike the Foundry, this property was alive and well.

“Your family was so well connected.” I marvel at his soon to be discovered lies.

"Isn't it amazing?"

A week later, Andrew is bringing a plethora of items to the Museum to share with staff and volunteers. Pictures of family members, stuff from his mother's basement in Ladue, including old pictures of his famous kin and silver trinkets.

His mother was quite the society maven. Attending the Ladue Club for luncheons, attending services at Ladue Chapel, but shopping less as she advanced in age and wasn't permitted to drive.

She started with a decent life, according to Andrew, "Mother was raised on a very prosperous farm in north central Illinois but married and divorced young with two children that became my older step-siblings. They then moved to St. Louis to live alongside relatives. To make extra money, she became a server at an upscale club and attracted the attention of my bachelor father. He was a self-made man with an impressive pedigree that worked his way up from an attorney to a judge, then retired to become a wealthy broker in Chicago. She became one of the upper crust."

Andrew's mother apparently knew one of the esteemed benefactors of several house museums, a woman whose husband had roots in a local car dealership that I'll call Jackie. Andrew claimed that his mother kept up with Jackie, and that Jackie's husband slept around on her for years. That the adulteress showed up at the car dealership for trysts. The front desk secretary and head salespeople were trained to warn Jackie's husband when Jackie was coming into the office with a code that "the shadow" was arriving.

If you think that this sounds like an amazing story, in truth, it's just that, a completely fabricated family history and tales of people that never met. The only things that I know that were true of the above, was that there is a farm, Andrew has parents, his father is a deceased former realtor, and he has two step siblings, and that there was a third son, a man Andrew never met, that his father reportedly adopted and abused before Andrew was born.

"Have you ever been to Lake Forest? I mean in Clayton."

“Yeah, I think, when I was a kid.”

“There are amazing homes we should check out.” I urge. “I used to work out of a house here, for a high-end handbag designer. I had my Hollywood fashion moment.”

I pull into the tony Clayton neighborhood.

“These are gorgeous homes. You can tell a bunch have been redone.” Andrew notices.

“Yep. Here it is!” We pull up in front of the English style manor. It still looked the same sans some trees. “I worked in the office up there, a room to the right. They kept the multi-colored diamond shaped stained glass.”

“What was that like?”

“Pretty cool. She had her Miranda moments. I was in New York during fashion week. I went to the Statue of Liberty, Ellis Island, and the Empire State Building. I thought about seeing the Twin Towers but I ran out of time. I took cool pics on the ferry to Ellis Island.” It felt like yesterday. “We were part of the Accessories Circuit in the Waldorf Astoria. Editors and reporters from the high end fashion magazines were in attendance. We were in the lobby peering at window displays when Trump walked by with his entourage. This is when he was married to Marla Maples.”

“That’s cool. You worked here?”

“Oh yeah, she had two sons in college. One was in Russia, the other out of state. Both super nice. Her husband founded one of the new tech companies.”

“You know, they sound familiar. I’m fairly sure we knew them. I was little but they had a wonderful Christmas party and Jake the younger son played with me and a train they gave me.”

“Really?” I wonder aloud. They were generous, popular donors to the St. Louis Art Museum with quite their own art collection in the house.

“They were good people.” He remembered.

“Yes they were.”

Months later I easily found holes in this story. My former employers were Jewish. The only Christian holiday thing they did was to put up a generic gold tree once. And they took it down early because their cats jumped into it.

"Speed up!" Andrew forms his fingers into a cross as we drive by Lemp Mansion. "It's cursed!"

I cackle, amazed at his fear of his family's historic home.

"You should be scared," he chastises.

"Actually, I used to know the current owners. I was part of an arts collective that rented out the stables in the early 2000's. I've stayed the night twice with an ex-boyfriend and then led a couple of tours for one of the ghost companies. We did a photo shoot in the Lavender Lady's room. I felt it was pretty creepy, but nothing personal happened to me."

We went along Benton Park. "My brother lives somewhere around here." Andrew called his sister out of the blue for details, but she doesn't know. I can tell she's a bit surprised that he contacted her. We gave up and headed towards Lafayette Park.

"You hate confrontation." Andrew chastised as we gazed at the stunning painted ladies of the rehabbed neighborhood.

"Probably true." I muse aloud.

He digs in. "You didn't get along too well with your dad, did you?"

I am blown away that he picks this up and pause for a moment. I hadn't spoken a lot about my father. My dad had quite the temper, but he was also kind and generous, a spiritual man. He'd been a driver or in construction for the majority of his life, from a beer truck to a cement mixer to a cabbie when things were rough, to a cemetery foreman and retiring as a teamster with a new cement company. He stopped drinking and smoking in his early 30's and was a pretty devout Catholic. With age and wisdom, I realize he didn't quite know how to handle a talented child prodigy daughter that could draw before she could talk and had the reading comprehension of a high school senior in third grade. He mellowed with age and became an awesome grandfather.

"He had anger issues. I still loved him but I was a momma's girl." I manage to deflect. I am suddenly acutely aware that Andrew's getting a too close for comfort emotionally. Which is strange because he's been like another brother.

This abrupt intrusion feels wrong and I don't know why. I resolved my feelings about my father long ago. I wished my mother had outlived him, but her diagnosed battle with MS began when I was only about ten years old. Even as a child I was an empath, I still feel absolutely everything. I have to set boundaries to this day. I understood then that mom's life was going to be shorter. It sucked.

I don't show a lot on the surface. But I don't want to shut off the emotions, as I've always believed it made me a better artist. So, I channel it into my work.

I will realize that this ability to sense that something was off, saved me from further emotional damage, but Andrew still gathered enough information about everything and everyone I knew to hurt me.

8 CLEANING HOUSE

"When an unpure spirit comes out of a person, it goes through and places seeking rest and does not find it. Then it says, 'I will return to the house I left.' When it arrives, it finds the house swept clean and put in order."
-Luke 11: 24-25

"If I die, remember, get over here and clean out everything, don't tell anyone." Andrew hands me his apartment key as we tidy up and organize his collection and apartment. This project started shortly after I helped him buy the bed.

"Can you help me clean up? I can pay you. I know you're talented at organizing. My family is coming over for snacks in a couple weeks." The text came over. I could use the money with the holidays coming and decided to help him out.

I arrived on a cool early autumn eve and we headed over to a huge strip mall to get cleaning supplies. We end up in what seems to be the biggest department store ever. When we leave, I'm already exhausted from his frequent distracted pauses. Once we arrived at his digs, we carry in the cleaning haul. I'm still impressed by his apartment, in a brand new development.

"How did you manage to get such a nice space so fast?" I hated to ask, but I was curious.

"I slept with the property manager." He winks.

“Okay,” I drawl with a knowing smile. I cannot get over how he charms everyone.

“I want you to meet my family, they’re coming over for dinner.” Andrew sounds both excited and anxious. I think, *okay, so that’s changed to dinner.*

At first look of Andrew’s place, you feel like you’ve walked into a micro museum. His apartment is decorated with a mix of Rococo to Edwardian décor. A curio cabinet is filled with figurines. There’s five or six Victorian and Eastlake style chairs and a fabulous poppy red jacquard print couch. I’m not a thin woman and he’s well over six feet, so when we sat on it together, we took up most of the space.

Before I even came over the first time, he warned me about how much stuff he had. And to be fair, I’m an artist, crafter, and costumer, who has moved galleries, shops, and storage spaces six times in seven years for various reasons. In three instances, married owners divorced and closed businesses/properties, but that’s another story. I had my own move coming up the following spring and dreaded it. I’ve also moved a couple of shops and businesses I’ve worked for, so I know the challenge of getting things in order. My version of hell would be waking up to having to move every day.

There are boxes of statuettes, lamps, books, clothing, suitcases, photos and paintings, including several by Louise Lemp, a noted artist and his ancestor. For the next several hours we do battle over the clutter.

I first condense the piles of clothing in his closet to make room for the paintings so that they’re not stacked alongside his bed, dresser or couch in his bedroom. We pull out trunks (“these were my family’s Louis Vuitton cases”) to put them on display or use them for storage in the closet. We neatly stack what won’t be put out on shelving.

Once the closet was done we tackled the cabinets and made room for vases, trinkets, and cookware. We thinned out his collection, picking out give-away and sell items. There’s a sizable pile of trash and recycling that went to the dumpster. We emptied a couple boxes, wrapping up about four hours of work but a second visit was necessary.

I returned to help him unload boxes and storage tubs full of mostly historical items. We reorganized the furniture in the living room to create additional sitting space and pick through another eight containers worth of stuff. We hang Louise's paintings, plus others he'd bought or collected. We add items to the curio cabinet and more to storage in the closet. We set up lamps and put out his best coffee table books. We clear out the coat closet and the cabinets to supply space for books not on display. We sort more things to sell, as he says he has a friend in Wisconsin who sells his cache on eBay for him because, "I don't know how to do that stuff." At one point we pause and Andrew begins pulling out family pictures and heirlooms.

"This is a family infinity ring. I usually keep it in a safe deposit box." The flashy diamond and gold band fits neatly on his pinky. "I only keep it for special occasions. Hey, I know you like this watch." The watch is a stunner, a slinky matte linked gold band and beige face. "It belonged to my grandfather and my dad passed it to me." We research this and a plethora of other goods as we put his collection in place. If the watch is truly the brand it says it is, it's worth close to ten thousand dollars.

"Did I tell you I have a Rolls Royce? It's stored on the family farm?"

"You're kidding?"

He pulls out pictures and video, plus others of him at the farm. One in particular strikes me in a bad way. He's outside a building holding a large assault rifle. He must've noticed my dismay because he notes, "I can't have guns anymore."

"Because of your mental state? You said you're on meds."

"Hmm, yeah. I told you I've been hospitalized twice, right?"

He'd alluded to it, and I felt it rude to ask, but he did say that after he and Curt divorced, he was driving near the family's farm property and totaled his car with the intention of killing himself. He was in the hospital for weeks, and not with just physical injuries. I'm not totally surprised by this admission. I noticed the crick in his nose and a scar over his lip hidden by his mustache.

"So, you've seen everything, I want you to be the executor of my estate."

I think he's joking. "Okay," is all I manage to say.

"The ring, the Rolls, the paintings. I have a key for you to the apartment. If I die, clean it out asap. Sell it. Any money left will go to my friend Margot's daughter. They don't have a lot unlike Tabitha."

He then proceeds to tell me about Margot, the first female friend that helps him with basically everything.

Margot will be the standard for the other women he uses in the future. I would be his "Margot" for a spell, another volunteer at another institution will be a Margot, overlapping with me, and the current gal that I know of is Abby (as of this writing and more on forthcoming). Each Margot is similar in that they are usually single, divorced or women unhappy in their marriages, they are not necessarily wealthy, but are somewhat connected, talented and/or intelligent. They are kind, generous, practical listeners, and enjoy his company, knowledge, and off-the-wall humor. His treatment of the Margos is the same: flattery and swift kindness, showered with attention, used for their knowledge and connections to make inroads to others, gains sympathy for his mental conditions, then eventual sharp endings due to his multiple deceits.

The original Margot was his first sidekick, but her homespun roots weren't good enough for him. Margot also married a guy he didn't think much of. They all lived together for a year or two.

"She was fat. Nice, friendly, but thick," Andrew remembers.

"But she was pretty?" I offer.

"No. She was ugly," he snickers.

I am still shocked at how nasty he can be. I saw a picture of Margot later, and she was a girlish kind of cute, which made me despise him more.

He told me how he moved onto Tabitha, who's family had roots in his hometown but relocated to St. Louis. She was model attractive and high maintenance. They moved to Chicago to live lake side, where they embraced the high life. But Tabitha got pregnant, never married the father, and left to her own space in Lake Forest.

"Tabitha won't talk to me anymore. I believe Margot's child deserves it. I'll have it written up after I consult with my attorneys. You have to promise to do it."

"I will, but understand, I'll need a stipend to fund the sales and organization of everything." I think fast. I used to be employed by a trust company. I don't want to be financially burdened with distribution fees and expenses.

"Louise's pieces are amazing." He changed the subject, pointed out each piece, told me the history of who they were, pulled out an auction booklet from when they were sold. He shared how he met her caretaker and bought a bunch of family items. "And like the other Lemps, she killed herself. Her husband died, and she wouldn't live without him."

"Have you ever considered doing an exhibition? I mean, you have so much Lemp stuff." We sort through tons of pictures and letters, including ones from family excursions to the Serengeti. I read a couple of them aloud. They are an astonishing historic glimpse into the upper crust life.

"Let's put these on TikTok! But we can't show your face. Just read aloud. I mean, we could make some cash." He exclaims.

"I'd have to think about it." At that moment I'm overwhelmed with the barrage of stuff, the history. "I mean, we can, but it'll take a bit, we'd probably have to create its own page. I don't have the time at the moment."

"Look at this, read it," Andrew hands me a letter he wrote as a kid about polishing the silver and watching Antiques Road Show with his mother and grandmother, "See! I was always like this."

The script is written on old school lined newsprint in crayon alongside stick figures. I do laugh out loud at the absurdity of it all.

"Can you cook? Like scones, tea, tea sandwiches for the party?" He asks eagerly, to which I agree.

We continue to clean and unbox the remaining items, spending about three hours organizing. We wipe and dust everything. The brief tangent of stopping to read over his family's letters and to look at photos was eye opening. I am grateful that Andrew seems relieved when we're done. "I can get a hot guy I know to hang curtains." He jokes as I leave.

A day or two later Andrew texted that he decided to buy food instead of having me cook. I then backed out of the apartment event as I'm wiped out. At that point I'm working four to five days a week in the city and weekends at the museum. On top of it all, I feel a cold coming on.

The day after when I texted him on how things went? He tells me his family didn't come over to the apartment, they decided to do dinner instead. He never did pay me for any of the work. I will always wonder if he had me do all that stuff to impress a high class attorney he was having a fling with. The key to his apartment wasn't given out of care or generosity. It was to cover his obsessions and lies.

And as always, I felt on an odd disparity in our friendship rising.

9 A CHANGE OF SEASONS

"and do not give the devil a foothold."
-Ephesians 4:27

"The old ladies like me," Andrew has bragged. But it's true, women over fifty adore him, women over seventy want to make him family. Andrew appears to be the full package. Tall, handsome, pedigreed, impeccable taste, knowledge of art and antiques, charming, polite, and the right amount of wit to those who haven't uncovered his past.

"You're off today? I have to drop something off at the Museum." He texts. "I don't want to bother anyone."

"I can. When?"

"About thirty minutes."

"Okay, meet at the side door entry, text when here." I am slowly getting started for the day. I only work two to three days a week for the Tea Room, but they are sometimes ten to twelve-hour days. On those days off, I used to crash. I threw on a tee shirt and leggings and texted the Museum that I'm coming over to get mail.

A half hour later, Andrew texts that he's at the door. I waltz through the downstairs of the gift shop of the Museum. The director stops me as I pass, "Hey, can I get your help for a minute?"

"Oh, Andrew is dropping by…he's at the door." I freeze. *Why do I suddenly think I'm in trouble?*

"We could use him too." He smiles and waves inside the door. There's a smattering of volunteers in the break room. "Come in."

I hurry and grab Andrew at the door. "Hey, we're getting pulled into a meeting."

"What?! Shit." Andrew groans. "What for?" He goes pale.

We had nothing to worry about. We were pulled in to assist in planning a benefit tea party. Over the next thirty minutes, the group produced a plan to hold a fabulous soiree that eventually, will not happen. For me, my concern was that I was spending too much time in the Museum off business hours or I was goofing off on the job. I'd realize later, that for Andrew, he had thought he was caught as an impostor.

"Are you OK?" Andrew picks me up in the Mercedes from the Tea Room two weeks later.

"Yeah, I will be." I drop our snacks in the back seat and climb into drive. Bea, my coworker and her spouse are leaving. They're a fab goth couple, he deejaying at local clubs, and she baking and creating some of the best knitted gothic goods I'd ever seen. As we pull away, by the looks on their faces I have that rotten feeling that something else is still wrong, even though I had already received horrible news. The London Tea Room on Locust was closing.

Bea and I were both incensed at the how the Tea Room was being shuttered. The landlord let the building rot and dragged the owner through court. But I believe this glance meant something else.

Andrew picked me up to comfort me. I packed a bunch of snacks for the chat. We eat our picnic in Lafayette park as I tell him what happened. To make things increasingly difficult, I have a massive fashion show and a booth to run at the last outdoor festival I will ever do. I have to finish creating and packing in the next two weeks. I have been doing dance recitals all summer with the studio I hired to be my models. It's crunch time and I am stressed out with tension headaches.

Andrew demolishes his food as I tell him what happened.

"The closing is to be by October first if not sooner." I hurry to eat, as I hadn't had a chance for a real lunch break. I texted everyone about what happened right after I found out.

"Um, don't worry, you always seem to fall on your feet." Andrew's right, I adjust quickly. Two days later I already secured a job with the city downtown. He seems distracted and embarrassed to be with me in the park that afternoon.

I look like crap, wearing old clothes that I bake in. I have grease and food stains everywhere. He sounds sincere, but I have a feeling he's got a hookup nearby. So much for comforting.

"Whelp, I need to get to work." I have about ninety minutes of clean up to finish.

We stand to hug and its awkward. And looking back? We didn't hug a lot, and when we did, it was strange. I wasn't expecting a romance, just kindness. Of all the gay friends I've ever had, he was absolutely the worst in an embrace. Perhaps another red flag I should've paid attention to.

"Are you coming to Hannibal?" We're driving around a week later. I made time for Andrew in between preps for Big River Steampunk Festival.

"When is this thing?"

"Labor Day weekend. It'll be the last show I'm doing. I can't do outdoor events anymore. My body doesn't like the heat. But I am going out with a bang. This fashion show will be amazing."

"I dunno. I might." His indecision was a no, I just didn't know it yet. I would come to understand his gaslighting techniques.

The Festival went well. I was grateful for that opportunity, but I was focused on other things to accomplish. My final autumn and winter with the Museum was approaching. I'd move come spring 2025.

"I talked to my mom, and she said after all I'd been through, I should walk away. I quit today," he texted. It was a little over five weeks since the Tea Room closed. Andrew became increasingly stressed about his job at the drugstore. They were sending him everywhere to assist various stores and firing other management, as far south as Cape Girardeau and as far east as Springfield, Illinois. The company announced it was closing a high number of locations. He was feeling burnt out and harassed.

"You did?" I will always wonder if they'd fired him. Suddenly he calls and I answer.

"Yeah, it's me. I did."

"You must feel a lot better."

"I do, but do you think I'll find another job soon?" Worry heightens the pitch of his voice.

"Well, possibly. You've already started searching anyway, right?"

"Oh yeah. I put out ten applications already. I've got to return to upscale retail."

"You have money from your trust, right?" I thought, *if he can afford a near million dollar home, surely he has a backup fund.*

"Well, the stipulation is I have to have a job."

"Oooops."

"My mom will support me." He paused, obviously distracted. "Um hey, I'm taking a nap while I'm relaxed. Chat later," he hangs up.

The relief was temporary, the longer Andrew was out of work, the worse he acted, enveloped by the darkness of depression. I spent hours helping him find a new job. We had multiple conversations about possible employers. We researched the companies, the staff with whom he was meeting. We scouted out the interview locations.

For one job with a tony Frontenac retailer, he went to lunch and drove around with the recruiter to view historic homes in the area, including his parents' house in Ladue. I'd later find out that this woman (who was not a retail human resources exec) was afraid to have been in a car with him.

"How did you get so lucky?" He marveled at how fast I'd found work after the Tea Room closed.

"It's not luck, I busted my ass. I also quit corporate America ten years ago. I wasn't doing that backstabbing bull shit for no pay anymore. My creative heart can't take it." I sighed. He was in the worst position in multiple ways, including being out of a job and struggling from mental illness.

For months on end there were texts, emails, tests, quizzes, online and in person job interviews. He considered trying to find something part time with no avail. But we agreed that it would be harder to find an upper level management position and he may have to settle. He was getting knocked out of the competition early, often not getting past the first round of interviews. In a lot of instances, not hearing anything at all.

One evening I went over to his apartment and updated his resume, which is how I now know why he was out of work for so long. His resume was fabricated. Any reputable HR department could find that out with a few simple calls or contacts.

10 A SCARY SEASON

"Idle hands are the devil's workshop."
-Proverbs 16:27

"You know I don't believe in that shit."

"You don't know until you try it. I need you to focus." The earlier plans for that day changed completely. I was supposed to come over to his apartment to clean and organize. We ended up hopping over to Main Street in St. Charles and trying to juju the bad vibes out of a Lemp ring that he inherited.

"It's nice out, you want to get lunch first? I'm starving." He greets me at the door. "Or how about the bins?" He can never make up his mind and not working has made it worse.

We begin driving and after a false start of heading for an antique mall, we settle for Main Street and a stop at Steak n Shake. It is an absolutely gorgeous late September day and I'm looking forward to autumn. This would not be the first incident that plans would change.

October has always been my party season. My birthday is early in the month, autumn is my favorite time of year and I revel in anything to do with Halloween. I attend at least two regular events. The month fills up quickly with costume preparation and plans. This year I was doing Witches Night Out in Kimmswick and the Halloween Party in the Central West End.

Between working my new temp job for the city, museum and Halloween plans, I sensed that Andrew was feeling slighted. His struggle to find a job worsened. And although he'd been volunteering at the Museum and Little Shop Around the Corner, he was slipping further into depression. He looked at other places to fill his boredom, including Oakland House in Affton. He was calling Hawken House and the Sappington Houses too. He had to keep busy for his mental state. He wistfully spoke of moving home to Illinois.

I reached out to Abby to assist him, introducing them via text. Abby lived on the Illinois side of the river where her husband was a military contractor and she was studying for advanced degrees in the mental health field.

Later on, I'd realize that this is where the switchover happened, where Abby became the new Margot. And not only did Andrew draw Abbey in, but he had also lured in another woman in a similar position as I, in yet another cultural institution, and was attempting to create nefarious inroads with at least three other wealthy older women. He always said, "the old ladies love me." And they did until they found out the truth months later.

"I want to do something special for your birthday. Let's do the Ladue Club, or Ramsey's at the Four Seasons!" Andrew cooed as we perused the shops on Main Street instead of getting his apartment together.

We passed a witches apothecary and decided to drop in. The scented candles, herbs and incense filled the air with the promise of mysticism. Crystals glittered in the autumn light that filtered through the charming historic windows.

"Maybe you could hex the Lemp ring or something." Andrew joked.

"I'll try."

The Lemp ring was a pinky signet ring with the family crest. Engraved and worn from wear, I saw that it was a special piece. And although he claimed it was cursed, he continued to wear it even when I suggested he take it off, if it was that much an evil talisman. I bought a sage bundle and a mini cauldron. After shopping additional hours, we went to the apartment to sage and cleanse the ring. I cycle prayers, incantations and sage wafts over it, then I told him to put it away. I showed him how I manifested, giving him a journal, and even a massage to assuage his anxiety.

"Do you feel any differently?"

"Meh. I told you I didn't believe in it," he grumbled. "But I am relaxed."

The spell was broken. About twenty bucks in metaphysical gear and ninety minutes wasted. Whether you'd understand that the manifesting and healing worked or not, it wouldn't have helped, because within nine months, I'd find out that Andrew wasn't related to the Lemps at all.

I was excited as my birthday drew near. In 2024, it was on a Saturday night in early October. But as we closed in on the date, Andrew spoke of other plans. I had a gut feeling I was getting ghosted, so I contacted my best childhood friend of over forty-five years to see the latest Joker movie at a late show as a backup.

Andrew did take me to dinner but I was bookended between two dates or hookups. It was downgraded from a whole grand evening out at the Four Seasons to only dinner. He was freshly laid before we arrived at a place in the southwest neighborhood near seven, waited way too long and paid too much for food that wasn't that great, and we were gone by eight. He was more interested in the other guests arriving than chatting over dinner. I felt that he didn't care to be there and the magic of our friendship was likely dying. He was headed for another date afterwards anyway.

I didn't want to desert him. He was struggling terribly. I thought he had been so spoiled that he wasn't used to having to budget. His mental health was spiraling. But that night he was ambivalent. It was a waste of my time.

I was glad I'd made a backup plan. I was at the movies by nine. The new Joker musical was kind of depressing, but the acting and music was superior. The best part of the evening was hanging alongside my lifelong bestie who appreciated my harlequin makeup. It wasn't a complete bust, but I won't forget that dinner went from a possible five-star high end dining experience to eating a terrible delayed meal for less than fifteen minutes at an outdoor café.

"We should do something nice for Abby, her birthday is coming up soon. We should throw a party." We're driving around on a lovely evening before things get cold and crazy with the upcoming holidays. I'm also getting bored.

Andrew has become less impressed during our drives. A couple weeks before this afternoon, we did a drive by of Oakland House in Affton and hit up Cliff Cave Park. We stopped to enjoy the Mississippi River overlook at dusk. On the way out of the park Andrew received an emergency call from work that ended up taking an hour. I stood on the edge of the grass, on a turnout lot, trying to make the best of some late sunset photography as he argued on the phone to a coworker about another employee.

"I dunno, I have a lot going on. I need to finish my outfit for Witches Night Out. Are you coming to the Central West End Halloween?" I deflect. I haven't seen Abby in over a year. Not that I don't care, but I'll be with lifelong friends at the other October events and work is getting busy at both jobs. If Andrew wants to throw a party, he's doing himself and I can't attend. I plan for Halloween shortly after Christmas. Halloween has become more like the holidays without the stress of cooking, cleaning, and gift hunting.

"Maybe, I need a costume though." He sighs as if uninterested.

"I have a couple jacquard print rococo style jackets you could borrow if you wanted to be Lord Ladue. Probably a frilly shirt too."

"Yeah, I'll be a vampire. Hot Lestat."

"Are you doing the Twilight Tour at Campbell?" I try to gauge what he's genuinely interested in because I'm not backing out on anyone.

"I thought about it."

"You should. It's a lot of fun. The Mourning Society comes, the lights are low, the house has that haunted feel, and you learn a lot. I've considered joining their Society, they do a lot of cool events."

"They're creepy." He expands on certain members using words that are too cruel to repeat here. I am wondering why I am still friends with someone so catty, especially when I know a lot of the Society members personally after working the event for five years. “Let’s go somewhere spooky,” he commands.

“Oh, I know where.” We get to Jefferson Barracks Cemetery right before closing at dusk. We drive around briefly and I’m somewhat perturbed that we can’t get to the oldest section that includes a stunning view of the Mississippi and Downtown St. Louis in the distance. The deer are out, nibbling at the remains of floral displays. Again, he seems bored.

“The park is still open too.” The Barracks Park is available to drive through and I show him the multiple museum and historic sites. We drive to another overlook and pass through the gate made of cannons and rifle barrels.

“Those deer are awfully close to the car.” He panics.

“They’re not bothering us,” I attempt to soothe.

“Don’t hit them.” His voice rises.

I sigh, I’m not even doing ten miles an hour.

“I want to go somewhere,” he moans. “Something scary.”

“You were just afraid of the deer.” I snicker as we get back onto the highway. “Okay, I know. Mini road trip to Alton.”

“No.”

“Yes, you want to see some stuff, we’re going.”

He pouts the whole way up to Alton, doom scrolling.

“We have to pass by the cemetery and see the Lovejoy Monument. It’s amazing,” I enthuse.

“Why are there so many potholes? God, I’m ready to go home.”

“Let’s drive by the McPike Mansion. It’s super haunted.”

“Okay,” he concedes.

We arrive at McPike minutes later where their Halloween open house is in full swing. Cars line the streets and a nearby parking lot is packed. A roaring bonfire has hordes of people sitting around hay bales. The house is appropriately decorated and the yard is filled with Halloween revelers.

"Let's get out." I'm excited as all hell. I'd been once before. The atmosphere is electric.

"No, I'm tired." He pouts. "Take me home."

"Just for a minute?"

"If you stop the car, I'm gonna leave you here."

"Okay, but a quick stop." I wanted to pass through Alton Park to see the Mississippi and St. Louis from a distance at night, but I cave. Andrew's wearing the crabby pants.

He leans the seat back and falls asleep on the way home. I glance over at him at one point and think, *what a beautiful disaster*. He awakes shortly after we get close to downtown St. Louis.

"We're almost at the Museum. You can sleep more."

"Um, I'm awake." He sits up and immediately checks his phone. "I have to get home anyway."

"Okay, no worries." For once, I am not the least bit tired. But his grumpiness is exhausting.

"What are you doing this weekend?" Andrew texts.

"I'm doing Witches Night Out, Saturday." It's mid-October and my Wicked Witch costume is nearly ready. I even have the green makeup and my Ozian green glasses.

"You going out after?"

"No, it ends late and then we get food. And I have to work the Museum the next day." I'm not in the mood to be persuaded otherwise.

It is unfortunate that Witches Night Out is kind of boring that evening. It started out well, but my friends usually win something and didn't even get into the costume contest finals. To top it off, someone stole my sunglasses.

I tried to look forward to the Central West End Halloween and the Twilight Tour at Campbell.

Campbell is fun as usual. The crowds get into it and the Mourning Society are authentic educators. Andrew doesn't go and seems disappointed that I do. It's technically not part of my job, but the Museum always needs assistance, and I've always liked this event. He could pout all he wanted. And yet again, the truth came out as to why he wasn't there. Most of the Mourning Society members were well aware of his fraudulent past from Chatillon-DeMenil and Lemp Mansion. He was afraid of being discovered.

I'm ready for the final event of the month, the Central West End Halloween. It's a massive event, (one year reported up to ten thousand people) crammed into a huge intersection. The costume contest is epic and I've been fortunate enough to be a judge representing Johnnie Brock's Dungeon twice. We've rented a table at Culpepper's in the past and was sticking to the only other close to the stage option, which was Kingside Diner.

I'm navigating my costume, putting on makeup, texting multiple friends, giving out last minute directions, when Andrew calls and we text back and forth.

"Why Kingside?"

"It's the only place close to the stage that has food and room for us." We have seven in our group, so I'm exhausted getting the right info to everyone. He decides not to come an hour before meetup. For someone that claimed to want to meet my friends, he was backing out a lot. And I was ticked that I wasted time digging out costume pieces for him.

The rest of us arrive at Kingside by six. The night kicks off with costumed people watching and great conversation, until the food comes out. We're already halfway through our two hour window, when a friend's order is screwed up. It will be another forty minutes before it's corrected. Abby and her husband came and immediately wondered where Andrew was. They are soon hammered and Abby goes on about her multiple surgeries, especially her breast implants for the remaining hour. When our time is up, we're unceremoniously booted out. The other tables are empty. We're pissed. It's cold.

Abby and her husband leave to wander the crowd. The rest of us sit at open tables for the end of the contest at Starbuck's patio. It's official, this Halloween season has sucked. I'm not feeling it at all. I can hear Andrew's voice in my head "Fucking Kingside Diner." As we head for our cars, I have the early signs of laryngitis.

By the end of the 2024 presidential election, I have the worst laryngitis virus. The whole team at work has it and we're exhausted. It was a harbinger of things to come.

11 DAYS & NIGHTS OUT WITH RAMSES

"Thou shall not make unto thee any graven image..Thou shalt not bow down thyself to them, nor serve them.."
-Exodus 20:4-5

"Let's call him Ramses!" Andrew holds a broken Egyptian figurine he picked up from one of his other volunteer posts. "They were pitching it. Do you think it's legit?"

"Possibly?" We scroll through archeological and historical websites and find similar pieces. "I remember seeing them in ancient art history class."

"He's gonna be our mascot, we'll take him everywhere! We'll start a social media show, Adventures with Ramses!" He beams like a child on Christmas morning.

"We'll get a TikTok page." I enthuse. "But we need to find out if he's real first."

"That'd be hilarious, we're driving around with a million-dollar find." He pauses briefly and changes the topic, "Hey one of the volunteers is throwing a party in Ladue, wanna go?"

"What's happening?"

"It's for the volunteers. About ten guests. Want to be my plus one?"

"When is it?"

"In a few weeks."

My autumn is already packed. "Let me see what my schedule is. If it's a Saturday or Sunday day I can't make it, I have to be at the Museum."

"You can't ask off?" He pouts. I wonder why he's scared to attend these events alone.

"No, I've already scheduled my remaining days off for the year. Let me know when they settle on a date."

"Do you think I should show some of my family pictures at the Museum? I'd like to find out if anyone knows anything." Another change in topic. There are moments when talking to him is like babysitting a four year old.

"Sure, there's a lot of volunteers that know a lot."

A short while later…

"This is my mom in Palm Beach." Andrew is showing off stacks of pictures of his famous families to another volunteer, Tony, a knowledgeable St. Louis historian, and a smattering of others. Tony was the volunteer that pulled up outside the Tea Room the first day we had tea. The pictures are loaded full of celebrities, Frank Sinatra amongst them. "I need to ask you about this one in particular." Andrew hands him a black and white photo of a home interior. Tony scans over it.

"It doesn't appear like it'd be in that house you were looking at." Tony seems skeptical as he glances at the exterior photos. They page through a small suitcase of pictures as Andrew grins from ear to ear.

Three days later we're volunteering and Ramses comes along for the ride. We show him coming in the front door and into the parlor. After our video adventure we go downstairs and chat as the tours come through.

"Do you think I should contact Bellefontaine about my families?"

"Well, their historians are amazing. It's a possibility. But you know Tyler and Dave are married."

"Hmmph," he snickers, his desire for Tyler still evident. "What about trying to get into the Antiques Road Show?"

"I'm a PBS member and entered the raffle. They're not announcing a decision until March." I want to be a part of this event in the worst way.

"What would you bring?"

"I'm not sure. I'd love to bring furniture, but that's crazy. Perhaps some of my Patrick Nagel prints. You?"

"Louise's paintings. Or Ramses, of course."

The afternoon drags until we close. He hangs a little too close for my comfort to the gift shop register as I shut down the Museum.

"Can't you do this later?" he whines.

"I'll be just another minute." I scowl. "This needs to be done."

"You're such a people pleaser."

"I'm just doing my job." I don't waver. The Museum is full of priceless items. I'm not letting it get broken into on my watch. He wanders off to the break room as I double check the doors and turn off the last lights.

I soon catch up to him. "Okay, ready?"

"Yeah." We head out to the car and bring Ramses out for an evening jaunt.

"You know we should call an archeologist or scholar to find out about Ramses," I google and find one at Washington University while at a stoplight.

Andrew emails them and gets a response after the weekend. I suggest that Andrew ask for a price, and the expert says he can't as it's a conflict of interest. "We need to investigate further," I push him to find out the truth.

But that doesn't stop Andrew from taking Ramses around town. His next adventure was the SLAM Friday night at the Art Museum, posing Ramses in front of paintings and visiting his ancestral sculptures in the Egyptian section.

"Doesn't he look like one of them?" Andrew peers into the case and then shoots photos for comparison.

"He does. But he could also be piece from a gift shop somewhere." This might be really bad or really good.

I run into a friend that's a practicing medium as we're getting ready to leave. We speak briefly as she's on her way to a special musical performance in one of the halls.

"Do you know everyone?" He smirks.

"Hmm, maybe." I shrug. *I have a lot of friends. What is his problem?*

We head on over to Square One Brewery for dinner afterwards. The weather has been warm but it's cooled off after the sunset. We share an immense bowl of chili which turns out to be too spicy, but the waitress noticed before we did and brought us a more edible batch.

"Make a video! Say the chili is too hot for Ramses," Andrew crows.

I laugh and oblige, posting to TikTok.

"Hey, would you help me pick out a cake for that event in Ladue."

"Sure."

"I'm thinking about picking up a cake at La Bonne Bouche on Olive. Schnuck's may not be good enough." We compare prices between the stores and gaze over the extraordinary desserts and cakes. Andrew is spoiled for choice, he cannot decide.

"We should visit in person but the prices are too high. I want to do something nice for Mattie though." Mattie is another coworker volunteer at yet another organization. They are throwing the party at her place. "But I like this chocolate strawberry one with pink icing."

"It's cute. Classic, I couldn't eat it though." I can't even think of attending anyhow. I have to work for the Museum.

"But you love sweets."

"I'm allergic to strawberries. Not horribly, I break out on my lips and the roof of my mouth. I'd have to pass on that. That is a pretty cake though." We proceed to another subject but I'm finding it disturbing how he gets obsessed on this stuff. I wonder who he's trying to impress. Why does he value my opinion so much? And why does he suddenly think it's too expensive?

On Monday, a couple weeks later Andrew texts when I'm at work, "She loved the cake!" A pic comes over and Andrew did purchase the chocolate strawberry. "Hardly anyone showed up but we had a good time."

I'm in a gray area where I'm glad he had fun, but I kind of didn't care. I'm beginning to plan for the upcoming holidays. My mind drifts to the party and Mattie, who he is raving about. I get the sense that he's collecting us ladies. My gut is not wrong.

"Want to go to the volunteer party at MoBot next week?" Andrew asks as we work at the Museum.

"I'm working, but it sounds fun. You should go. They treat volunteers well."

"Caroline is going and wants to meet up, but she's kinda flighty."

"Go anyway. Besides, talk to the staff at Little Shop, you should be able to get in free. The Garden is amazing." We embrace other topics and go to bed.

The night of the party he calls. "You won't believe this. I had to pay to get into the event."

"What? Are you there now?"

"Just leaving. Caroline said she'd text me when she got here and never did. She's such a flake."

"That's weird." He sounds a little lit. I absently wonder if he was stood up for a hook up.

"I walked around for about an hour for nothing. There weren't even any guys to hit on. I'm gonna go home. But I have tickets to Glow, you want to go?"

"Sure! You should bring Ramses."

We end up chatting on the phone his whole ride home and planning the future soiree. In the back of my mind, I'm still wondering what really happened that night.

About two weeks later, we're at Glow at MoBot, getting ready to trot inside.

"Looky what I got." I give Andrew an early Christmas present, a malachite pyramid for Ramses.

"Cool."

"This will be fun!" It turns out to be the employee and volunteer appreciation party as we check in. I briefly wonder what that other party was about.

We're not even through the new entry way when I run into former coworkers from when I worked at the Garden Gate Shop. We chat briefly as Andrew is distracted by the Christmas trees. He's not in the mood to be introduced.

"Hey, let's get pictures of him and the tree," Andrew suggests and I leave my former team members. "Who don't you know?" he protests as if envious of my numerous friends.

"Calm down, let's get Ramses in the tree." It's hysterical. He's cute by the massive gold ornaments.

"Okay enough, let's go, you move so slow," he prods.

The temperature outside is amazing as we walk out onto the main courtyard. The Glow is incredible as always. I pause with Ramses in the brilliant displays. We're at the lily pond lined by the musically timed lights, not even a fourth of the way through the show, when I notice that Andrew is already bored.

“Did you want any hot cocoa? Or a drink?” I suggested.

“Not really.”

He begins his endless scrolling on his phone as we walk along the vividly colored décor. Each time I stop to get pics of Ramses he gets further ahead. I catch up near the Tower Grove House.

“You should see this, they have the neatest video on the house.” I’m always impressed by this part of the Glow. I finally get him to sit on a bench and watch it.

As soon as it’s over he stands and leaves. I give up. I shoot more pictures on the last leg return to the entry way because a radiant moon is out and I can’t resist. I’m trying to be grateful, but I’m not dealing with moody Andrew very well. A wave of melancholia washes over me. *How sad that he’s not enjoying any of this beauty.*

By the time we leave, I’m regretting I gave him the pyramid. Another of the gifts bestowed on him in error.

12 A POSH THANKSGIVING & MEETING MARIAH

"Your adversary the devil prowls around like a roaring lion, seeking someone to devour. Resist him, firm in your faith.."
-1 Peter 5: 8-9

"We got a lot of food." Andrew laughed as we stuffed his refrigerator and cabinets on the night before his birthday. I brought most of what we'd needed but we still popped off to the grocery store for last minute items. I over packed everything, clothes, jewelry, food, pans and cooking utensils. We had the trappings of a grand Thanksgiving and birthday feast spread over three days.

I was making up for lost time. I was knocked out with laryngitis for two weeks after the Presidential Election in early November. Andrew made a trip to Milwaukee and an extended visit to the family farm near Bloomington, Illinois. We did a planning meeting drive a week or two before. We were celebrating his fortieth in style.

"Mother was pulled over in Ladue."

"What?"

"She ran a red light, and well the officer pulled her over and chastised her. She's not supposed to be driving."

"Yeah?"

"Didn't I tell you? She has a driver. A black man, just like the movies."

"You're kidding?"

"No. He has a limo and drives her to the farm. He's getting kind of elderly though. They argue a lot."

"That's hilarious."

Even though I was exhausted and still fighting to get my voice back to one hundred percent, I vowed to make Andrew's 40th birthday memorable. His 30th hadn't ended well. Friends threw a grand party for him and other family members for a week at a famous local estate home and he was violently sick at the end.

"I drank too much." He mused aloud. I'd later find that this statement was the only thing that was true about that evening.

This year, his birthday fell on Thanksgiving, and thus the plans kept evolving. First he was going to Savannah to meet with friends that were throwing him a party alongside a famous author. Then he invited me to Thanksgiving at a private club in Ladue with his mother and other family members, then it changed to possibly driving to his family's farm in Illinois. When that didn't happen, he was stressed about being alone, although with his penchant for finding available men on Grindr, I wasn't sure he was going to be lonely for long. This became another Andrew "MO" memory for me: make plans, make grander plans, end up doing most of the planning and Andrew wouldn't pay for anything. Or the worst case scenario, nothing happened at all.

The night before Thanksgiving, we ate microwave and finger foods for dinner and set up a table in Andrew's living room, resplendent with his family's silver. "Doesn't this look amazing?"

"Yeah!" We covered up a card table with family linens as well. It was impressive.

"Let's have a tea on the bed and watch movies!" We set up a mini tea service on his fabulous bed and watched a colonial era classic of gossip and retribution. Andrew was caught up in the drama. "Have you seen that new Truman Capote movie about his relationship with the wealthy socialites? It's like a modern version of this," he gushed.

"I haven't, but I saw the previews. It looks interesting."

"Oh, how he plays these catty bitches." I now find it ironic that he revered these movies of rumors, lust, adultery, and scheming.

After the movie, he went on and on about Tyler, the husband of David, another employee of another storied historical institution in St. Louis. "I'm gonna break up their marriage," he exclaimed with the kind of bravado a Lothario would exhibit.

"Stop." I'm horrified because I know he's not kidding.

"Dave is an old man." He sneered. "Make sure to post the tea party on social media. I bet he'll see it."

"Sure." I do create and post a quick video, but frankly I'm disturbed at this sudden obsession. Tyler is attractive, and Dave has the demeanor of an old school gentleman. They have been together for decades. They're good men. They volunteer for multiple organizations. I don't foresee Andrew getting close to either of them let alone getting between them.

After the tea was put up, I slept on the Victorian couch in Andrew's living room, exhausted, hoping I'd have enough energy to pull off the plans I developed for the whole weekend. Overnight a bitter cold front came through. I did not want to get off the couch.

The next morning, I made brunch while Andrew took a shower. We planned on croissants, eggs, and bacon. I began cooking and sang show tunes. But the bacon didn't fry well, it was dry as fuck, and when I added water to the bacon (he didn't have any cooking oil). A gust of steam and grease smoke went up and set off the smoke alarm.

"You trying to set fire to my place!" Andrew bounded into the kitchen as the rapid beeps of the alarm started.

"Hit the button!" I yell.

"What button?"

"On the smoke alarm, up there. You're tall, you should reach it."

"I can't." Andrew panics.

I grab the step ladder and practically fling it at him. "Press the button."

He climbs the ladder, taps the alarm, it stops and starts again. "It's not working."

"You have to hold it for a few seconds!"

"Ugh." He finally gets it to stop.

"Okay, now open the windows," I am terse and tired.

"The bedroom ones are blocked. And I don't want to mess up my curtains."

I swear if anything was going to kill Andrew, it would be vanity.

"Crack open the patio door, hit the ceiling fan, and AC," I mumbled.

After several minutes, the fog of bad bacon clears.

"You don't put water in hot grease. And stop singing Evita." He snarls.

"Shush. Breakfast is basically done. It'll be a minute to scramble the eggs. Quit whining and sit." I swiftly finish cooking and fill our plates. "Tea is ready. But this bacon sucks."

We sit down to eat.

"Yeah, this bacon sucks," he admits.

"It's crap. I bet it's composite shit. Who makes bad bacon?"

"Everything else is great. Thanks for making brunch. I didn't know you were doing this. When is the movie?"

"One thirty."

And thus, part two of Andrew's birthday extravaganza began. We dressed up to see the movie "Callas" as he adored opera. The temperature began to drop further as we headed to the movie theatre in Frontenac Plaza. As we pulled into the garage, he was actually excited. It was nice to see the old Andrew back.

There were issues the minute we arrived. The parking garage elevator was broken. I resisted the urge to sneak in snacks, but I should've heeded my gut. The security guard waved us past the elevators and directed us to the stairwell. I tried not to trip on my dress as we clomped up the stairs. "Well, this sucks."

A water pipe burst a couple days before at the theatre and they couldn't serve food at the concession stand.

"What the fuck is this?" Andrew grumbled as we each received a puny cup to procure water from the drinking fountain in the mall. The gal behind the counter shrugged. I'm officially pissed that I didn't smuggle in anything. At that moment, a chub of wine would've been dandy.

Once inside the theatre, I immediately noticed that the back rows were cordoned off due to snow-melt dripping in from the ceiling.

"Holy shit." Andrew mutters. "Head for the front so I can hear."

We settle in and begin to watch the movie with a tiny band of others. I somehow manage to ignore the steady dripping from the ceiling tiles into the buckets behind us.

The film uses a lot of cinematography to make scenes visually vintage including unsteady shots, black and white, technicolor and shadows. It is a peculiar shadow that causes a cackle of laughter from the crowd as it suddenly crosses entire the screen from a soaked ceiling tile that blocked the film and cascaded to the floor in a crash behind us. Everyone looked at each other incredulously and twittered.

"What the fuck?" Andrew chortles. I laugh so hard I nearly pee in my pants.

And it is chilly. I'm not normally that cold, especially living through perimenopause, but by the end, I am uncomfortable and hungry.

"Let's get out of here." Andrew mumbles as soon as the credits end.

"Yeah."

We sit in the Mercedes trying to warm up and make plans.

"Do you know if Oak Grove is open?" Andrew perks up. "It's too early for dinner."

"Yeah, hold on." I search for it online. "Yep, open until sunset, we have time, only fifteen minutes away."

"I need a snack." We decide to dash to QuikTrip for snacks before heading to Oak Grove Cemetery where a sculpture from the Campbell collection is displayed in the main mausoleum.

"I don't want anything, maybe alcohol." He pouted and remained in the car.

I come out bearing a soda and chips, and I grabbed him a beer that he doesn't drink. He proceeds to eat a bunch of the chips anyway. I try not to fume as we get to the cemetery.

I'm surprised that cars are parked near the front gates which are wide open. This is more comforting than a few weeks before when we passed by on a foggy cold dark night. There weren't any lights on the grounds and it was pitch black. We didn't dare go in that night.

"That has to be the mausoleum." He pointed to an impressive building on the right hand side of the grounds. It is a stunning piece of architecture with stained glass windows and a pair of lions guarding the main entrance.

"God, it's cold." I mutter as we walk around. As the sun sets, the wind is picking up. We can't see anything inside, but we find pics online. The statue that belonged to the Campbells was impressive, an angel carrying a fallen soldier to heaven. We take a bunch of pictures. "I wonder how big it is, if we broke in and carried it off," he jokes.

Andrew later tells management at Campbell that he has contacted the cemetery and family members of the current ownership of the statue about returning it to the Museum. I will always wonder if he did any of that. And if he did call them, did Andrew really contact them for the Museum? Or for himself? Because there's another mausoleum he claimed to be a part of, and that is one of the events that hindered his charade over ten years ago.

We eat dinner late. As soon as we return from the cemetery, I commence cooking our feast. Thanksgiving dinner is pretty fabulous, salad, Cornish hens, stuffing, mashed potatoes, pies and ice cream birthday cake that unfortunately melted in the fridge (I thought it was frozen solid, it wasn't). We shoot a multitude of videos and pictures of the table setting, the food, the apartment, and of course Andrew wearing the watch and "family" rings, including the haunted Lemp signet ring on his pinky. Of course he wants me to post it everywhere. I oblige.

Despite cooking and driving around all day, I do commit to giving him a massage and ASMR to get him to sleep.

I spent another night sleeping on his couch. The next day we're seeing Mariah Carey's Christmas show at Enterprise Center but I could only get nosebleed seats. Before I fell asleep, I randomly imagined, *it'd be great to get front row tickets somehow.*

Andrew already agreed to work black Friday for Little Shop. So, he got up earlier and left to volunteer. It snowed a tad but the sky was clear before he left.

I cleaned the apartment, took a shower, gathered my stuff, and hurried to the Museum. I still marveled that he didn't know how to use the stove or dishwasher in his own apartment.

I'm bushed, so I attempt to nap at my apartment at the Museum. But they're packed full of visitors. I get up, grab a snack and get dressed.

"Ready for part three?" I smile as he pulled up to the Museum. We snack on leftovers before we walk from the Museum to Enterprise Center in the bitter cold.

Once inside, we're on the wrong end of the arena and walk to the escalator. I have to pause and get a drink, but the lines are long. I will regret this slightly later.

"Let's get to our seats." Andrew mumbles. He's jittery going up the escalator.

"Aren't you excited?" I squeal. This show has been on my bucket list.

"Hmm. Yeah." He darts around furtively as we find our section. We walk inside the entry curtain along a throng of other spectators. Andrew groans aloud. At first I think it's because the seats are way across from the center stage.

The usher shows us our seats. "Up there and over to the right." He points. We're only ten rows from the top of the arena.

"Okay, let's go." I'm ready to sit and let Mariah's goodness roll over me.

"I'm not going." He utters.

"WHAT?!"

"I can't, I'm scared of heights." He flipped out, paled, and walked off into the concourse.

"What, wait, are you serious?" I am flummoxed. I saw the panic in his eyes. *What the fuck?*

"Come on, you can do this. Follow me." He dragged his feet behind me. I strode halfway up the stairs to the seats and realized that I didn't see him behind me at all. I ran down. I was cold before but now I'm breaking a sweat.

"Nope, nope, I'm scared of heights." I find him practically hiding behind a beer cart. What's worse is he can't hear anything above the crowd around us and my voice can't keep up.

"Okay, let me see what I can do. Come on." I dashed to the usher, told him the situation, and we scurried to the box office to try for better tickets. Full disclosure, I had agoraphobia/panic disorder for about a six month period in my mid-teens after a horrible bout of strep throat. I know what a panic attack feels like. But I also feel that I really want to see Mariah and I am outta fucks.

“Where are we going?” Four-year-old Andrew is back as he lagged behind. “I mean, you practically burn down my apartment, the movie theatre is falling apart, what else could go wrong?”

“Come on,” I groaned, checked my bank account and made sure I had enough funds to swing better seats financially. After a short wait at the ticket window, I find out there is nothing available in the lower bowl at all.

“Now what. Did you spend a lot?” He grimaced.

“Yeah. Um, do you want to go home? You don’t have to stay. I mean…I’ll give you your car keys. Call me when you get to the Museum.” I decided I’m not leaving. He said he wanted to go to this show. I bought our tickets in August. I’ve been looking forward to this for weeks.

“Did I leave my keys in the Museum? Where’s my wallet?” He’s still panicked.

“Wallet is in your coat pocket. I have your keys in my purse.” I dug them out and was ready to hand them to him when he shocked me.

“Um, I’ll try.”

“You, sure?”

“Let’s go now before I change my mind.”

I lead him back up. This time he followed. The seats were incredibly uncomfortable which didn’t help matters.

“Just breathe.” I tried to engage him in other conversation through the opening DJ set. He loosened up near the end, singing along to the songs.

Suddenly I notice the usher pointing at us and holding up two fingers. I am beside myself with joy. We’re getting better seats.

“Come on! Grab your stuff!” I hollered.

“Where we going?”

“Come on!” I gleefully trotted. The usher remembered that I told him about Andrew’s fear of heights and he procured complimentary tickets downstairs for us. They flashed the lights that the main event was starting. I was practically running until we landed in our new section. We're finally in an area where he can hear. "We have front row tickets!!!"

At last, he smiles. We bound to our seats in the media section, front row along the railing to the floor. I am dying of thirst but manage to hold out for most of the show with cough drops and mints.

"I manifested this." I grin wildly as we took pics and the show began. Near the end, Mariah tells the crowd she can't do this for everyone, but she will come to the front row to greet people.

"Oh my God, oh my God, we're gonna meet Mariah!" I am flushed with excitement.

"Shut up. What?" Andrew is absolutely perplexed.

Five minutes later, Mariah is close enough to touch. She sweetly greets a section of ecstatic little girls next to us. I am over the moon. I am grateful to the universe that something went right. I practically float home to the Museum. It's a little rough to work the next day, but meeting Mariah made it all worth it.

Later, I found additional truths come to light about Andrew's thirtieth birthday, ten years prior. He essentially lied to the owners of the estate, was embarrassedly, insanely drunk, vomiting continuously at the end of the bash, and was asked to leave the next day. He reportedly spent a week with those victims.

I am beyond tired and struggling to retain my voice for the remainder of Thanksgiving weekend. But as always, Andrew took everything I gave and then some. I should've left something behind for myself, some time off. Because I'd be far more sick in just a few short days.

13 COVID & PERSUASION

"Fear the Lord and turn away from evil. It will be healing to your flesh and refreshment to your bones."
Proverbs 3:7-8

"You're always tired." Andrew griped as we spend an afternoon thrifting on a weekend shortly after his epic birthday. We'd been to the bins at Goodwill. It was a madhouse, full of pickers, Christmas décor and kids everywhere, on the floor, in and under the bins, playing with broken toys, a couple of them screaming at the top of their lungs. I can barely handle it.

Andrew has lost his patience with the hubbub as well, but for some reason is clinging to hope that he'll find something. There isn't much to see and it's one of the few visits I don't get anything. I'm also reminding myself that I am moving in four short months and don't need to have additional things to pack. I was hoping to have cleaned and organized my storage unit by now, but I'm out of time. The holidays are upon us. I wisely decide not to decorate. *Why put up more stuff to take down?*

"Let's go." He snorted and we exited. It was chilly and I was ready to leave. I'd already worked the Museum that afternoon. The holiday parlor tours were ramping up. Museum guests love a Victorian Christmas. Andrew and Abby worked an evening event.

By early December I was feeling like I was ready to start tackling my preps to move. I was on a serious apartment search. I began with two places in Lafayette Square but realized I couldn't afford either of them. I purposely didn't bring Andrew. I needed to focus and the likelihood of us moving in together dwindled.

We looked at a last house in Lafayette Square together. I knew the realtor from volunteering at other institutions, an excellent high-end seller. Andrew had said he'd dated him in high school (another lie). The house was stunning on the bottom front half, but the rest was too modern.

"I hate this grey. And they tore a wall down. Upstairs is like a high end department store with bad carpet." Andrew sniveled.

Something was off, my gut was unhappy.

One plus about working and living in the city is that home and both jobs are only three blocks apart. For months I saved on gas walking to and from work.

We had an arctic blast in the second week of December, a Tuesday with frigid temps, but despite the cold, I still walked to work on the day I first felt sick. I'd been feeling hot for a couple days as I was layered up but hadn't thought anything of it. The heat was blasting at work. I'd been around a lot of people everywhere.

On a break at the day job, I went to the bathroom to take off a turtleneck from underneath my sweater. I struggled to stay awake. I went straight home, picked at dinner and crashed into bed for a nap around six pm. Normally I do thirty-minute to hour-long naps, so when I awoke at eight thirty, burning up, I knew something was wrong. My temp was a hundred and four. I popped a couple Tylenol, grabbed some crackers and water and headed to bed. I awoke a few instances during the night and found that my fever wasn't receding at all. By morning I called in sick and took a Covid test. *It's positive, crap.*

I contacted the doc and found that my insurance wouldn't cover the whole of Paxlovid. I don't have twelve hundred (yes, $1,200) to shell out for this. I let various friends and family members know, including Andrew.

"I am so sick with Covid."

"I think I got it too." We commiserate via text. Only he feels better in forty-eight hours. I feel like I was hit by truck.

In the five years since Covid started, somehow I never caught it, at least with OTC tests. There were times I swore I had it, but multiple negative tests told me otherwise.

For the next five days, I slept, ate little, guzzled fluids and took copious amounts of various fever reducers that barely made a dent. I'd never run a fever this high for this long and I was scared. Friends and family dropped off food and fluids.

"You still sick?" Andrew texts after two days.

"Yes, I still have Covid. It's gonna be a bit."

"You getting up and around yet?" he persists.

"The doctor told me to sleep." *He is so fucking impatient. I can't fucking get out of bed.*

By Saturday morning I get the stomach portion, a sudden nausea that makes me sit on the toilet and hold a plastic trash can at the same time. The only beneficial part of this is that I am so sick that I've hardly eaten anything. Despite dry heaving for about five minutes, there's only a smidgen of water to come up. After about two hours and Tums, I make sure to sleep quasi sitting up in case I have to attempt to vomit again.

In the very late afternoon, the nausea abates, and I am able to stomach crackers and juice. I get the fever to under a hundred, but it still hovers around ninety-eight, ninety-nine for about four more days. I have a tinge of a sore throat, but my voice is gone for a third time in under four months. I possessed all the flu-like symptoms otherwise.

I am pissed. I still wasn't a hundred percent since the election. Andrew tried to call repeatedly and I text back. "I can NOT talk." So, he ends up texting three to four times a day. I want to be left alone. Finally, by the twenty second of December, I dash to urgent care and get a chest Xray scan and test negative for everything. I am given an inhaler and am cleared to see family and go to work. I literally needed to drive the three blocks to work because I could not walk more than ten feet without feeling exhausted.

My family has a small Christmas, it's fun, but my voice is hovering around fifty percent. I'm still sleeping twelve hours. I finish my meds. Andrew insists on calling, but I hold him off with texts. He's still out of work, I know his anxiety is high, but I can't deal. *Why is he so fucking needy?*

"You need to get out," he calls.

"I'm exhausted," I whisper.

"I want to peek at a house. Just a short drive?"

I am super hesitant, but Andrew's prodding convinces me I need fresh air. Christmas break temps are terrifically mild. I'm comfy in only a hoodie.

He picked me up and mused aloud, "Oh, you don't look good."

"Well, I am starting to feel better. I worked a couple short days."

We went to search a house in the Central West End, supposedly one his family owned. The neighborhood is not great and the streets are frozen over and slick with ice. We pop out and looked around as it seemed to be vacant. I am slightly lightheaded as we get into the car. I require fluids and a little food.

"Let's get something to eat, I'm starving." Andrew suggested. "Let's get something at Square One."

We headed over to our favorite spot and sit at what is almost always our regular table. Several of the servers are wearing masks as well as I. *I hope I never get that shit again*. I let him talk the whole meal, blathering on about failed app dating and antique shopping, the usual stuff.

Andrew spent most of the meal on my phone after I properly sanitized it. It must've have killed him not to have been able to look at Facebook for three weeks. Our food arrives, but I'm more tired than hungry.

"You done? Let's get this to go and hit up the bins," he's excited.

"I can't." I whispered. My voice sucked. It took every ounce of air I had to get any words out. Our server brought a to-go box and we headed to the car as the sun was setting. I am crashing.

He dropped me off at the Museum with one last attempt to change my mind, I refused, waved him away and went inside. I instantly lay down and fell asleep.

Andrew stopped by on the weekend between Christmas and New Years as I tried to work at the Museum. "Can we see the Christmas stuff? I didn't get a chance to see a lot during the parlor tour."

"Okay." We walked through the kitchen and butler's pantry. He paused to gaze at the Campbell family silver and china. "Do you have the key to these cabinets?"

"No, I don't. Probably the one key I don't have," I mumbled.

We proceeded to the parlor. Later I will wonder what he would've done if I'd had the key to those cabinets.

"Shit!" It's New Year's Eve Day and despite being terribly tired, I forced myself to get dressed for work. I was going to leave early at 2pm anyway and guess that I can hold out until then. But as I'm wrapping up my hair, I'm getting hot. I double check the thermostat and think *did I remember to turn down the heat*?

I muse that I might be having a hot flash, flop onto the bed, and begrudgingly decide to take my temperature. The thermometer beeps too soon for my taste because I am running another fever. It's not the skyrocket one hundred four that I developed before, but 99-100 is not healthy. I scramble for another Covid test and fifteen minutes later, wham, I have Covid again.

I call into work. I call the doc. And cry. "I cannot fucking believe this," I grumble to myself as I grab more Advil. I am quarantined for at least two weeks with another round of antibiotics, steroids and inhaler. I worry that my voice won't come back although sounding like Kathleen Turner probably isn't a bad thing for someone that does occasional voiceover work.

Covid is a fucking boomerang bitch.

The day after New Year's Day we have a hell of a snowstorm. The city basically shuts down for a week. I am grateful for two things, that I ordered delivery of soup and supplies and that I don't have to be anywhere while feeling like shit. The doc says I'm not leaving the apartment anyway.

The fever didn't spike like it did before but I definitely gained a sinus infection and my voice decided to disappear for another five days. On day three of this round, my face and neck feels like hell and I have insomnia.

Andrew calls two to three times a day. "You're still sick?"

I enjoy the concern and company, but I want to rest. "I'm not gonna get over this if I keep talking," I can barely tell him. Then he'd switch subjects and talk some more, further wearing me down.

On day four, I figure if my face still hurts this badly, I'm bringing out the heavy artillery. I call the doc again and ask if I should take the Tylenol 3 I was prescribed from my last dental procedure. And with that permission, I get pain relief and sleep. I had all the weird symptoms that round except for loss of taste and smell. I even experienced Covid toe and a light case of thrush from the meds.

By the end of this medical purgatory, I'd gone through ten Covid test kits, lost fifteen pounds and a lot of my sanity. I already had hair loss with perimenopause, but it worsened. Brain fog was a strange beast, I remembered my schedule, to get gas, and to set my alarm. I couldn't remember major actors and the movies they starred in. I was talking to someone about a popular old movie and it came out "that hot guy that's been famous since the 1980's, he was in that military movie with the planes."

Meanwhile, Andrew was snowed in, out of work and bored, still calling me for two to three hours at a stretch. I was worried my vocal damage was going to be permanent.

Andrew asked about the gay and club scene in the nineties in St. Louis, places where I worked, pictures of my grandparents and great-grandparents and trips I took. I caved and I texted. I shared a ton of pictures. He became slightly obsessed with a man I'll call Joe, who I knew in college and was a friend's first gay lover.

The friendship with Joe ended horribly. Joe was a liar too, but despite being a drug addict, he was never as bad as Andrew was. Joe's family had legitimate money. I ran into Joe years later when I was at a cell phone store where he upgraded my phone. By the way he spoke to me, I was confident he didn't remember who I was. For that moment of non-recognition and grace I was grateful. I hadn't thought of him in over fifteen years. I can't even fathom the idea of Andrew tracking Joe. Although knowing Joe's background, he'd probably be able to smoke him out.

I'd realize that Andrew pumped me for history on the club scene in St. Louis (and other things) to use that information for his own nefarious purposes. I wonder how many of my pics will be shown to other people to prove that he was here at those time periods.

I am struck by how much alike Joe and Andrew were, even twenty five years apart. I still have the same tastes apparently, but I'm wiser in a lot of ways. Joe never pretended to fawn over me.

The time I set aside to search for apartments and packing vanished. At the end of January, I scrolled through a multitude of listings but I lacked the energy to call. Places I'd hoped to see earlier had rented.

"Why do you have to move? Surely they'll let you stay. Abby says the same thing." Andrew tried to coax me into picking up stuff I didn't need and he certainly wanted me to stay at the Museum.

I was tired of reminding him that I must pack. My apartment looked like a bomb hit it after I had Covid and left me with persistent exhaustion. I was also starting a new job at an antique store.

Also repetitious explaining that my contract ended was tiring, the date decided long before Andrew began at the Museum. I'll never know if Andrew wasn't listening, if it was because of his hearing loss, or if he was so engrossed in his bullshit that he didn't care.

But of one thing I was certain, after the truth was told, of who he really was, was that Andrew wanted me to stay in order to have access to the Museum.

14 A TRIP TO THE CEMETERY & LAST DAYS AT THE MUSEUM

"For like the grass they will soon wither, like green herbs they will soon die away."

-Psalm 37: 2

"Holy crap it's cold." I'm layered in a turtleneck, a thick sweater and heavy coat and I'm still freezing in the bitter blast. We are standing on the Petring plot in Bellefontaine Cemetery. After suffering through Covid for two months, this is the last place I should be.

We were taking a regular Sunday drive. I should've been home resting or packing or both. He picked me up as usual.

"So, where we going?" I hopped in the driver's seat.

"I dunno."

"How about we see Jefferson Barracks? I can show you where my maternal grandparents are buried." We get inside and he's bored. We head to the bluffs desiring to see the historic headstones and unfortunately they are blocked off.

"Now what?" he groans.

"We could hit Bellefontaine," I suggest. I'm doing him this favor. I appreciated his kindness when I was sick, checking in with me, so I'm going, hoping it heals his depression as he's still out of a job.

Snow is still on the ground from a month before at Bellefontaine. A dusting fell overnight and it continued to flurry soft flakes around the grey stones of the deceased.

"They say the Petring's have the biggest plot because it's on a corner. Do you think you can find it?"

"I'm fairly sure. You know I don't like to give up. Remember how I told you about my friend Addison? When her ex-husband was having an affair, the only thing she knew about the other woman was her Insta handle. Within ten minutes of getting that information from Addison, I had that woman's name, age, her ex-husband's and child's names and when she was first divorced. Also, what area she lived in and where she worked. Which happened to be with Addison's then husband."

"Isn't that nosey?" Andrew seemed a tad concerned about this particular skill of mine.

"Like you aren't?" I wheeze, my voice still weak. I will discover why he seemed put off by my ability to research.

I use a combination of the iPhone maps app and a map off the Bellefontaine Cemetery website to guide us through the gothic beauty of the grounds. We drove past the Campbell plot and sped by the Lemp Mausoleum which freaked him out.

"Hurry! It's cursed!" Andrew gasped. I will later find out why he behaves this way around all things Lemp. We also found the Niedringhaus plot on the way. We pause and shoot pictures.

At last, the maps align minutes later.

"There it is!" Andrew bounds out. He knows the names on the stones, saying who is related to whom.

"You know, when I met with David, he told me I could get buried here because I'm a descendant. Do you want to get buried here?"

I giggle nervously. I considered that when I passed I'd like to be cremated and interred near my family, perhaps infused into a sculpture. My grandparents, parents, sister and my aunt and uncle are all buried in the same row at Resurrection in Affton. "I'll pass, thanks."

As usual, I document everything for him, taking some of the best cemetery pictures I've ever shot despite feeling like death myself.

But my time was wasted. Andrew wasn't related to any of them.

"Wow these are strong." Andrew sips from his bloody Mary at Soulard Market a couple weeks later. And the drinks are quite infused with alcohol.

We were at the Mardi Gras Pet Parade and as always, the pet parade weather on Sunday was incredible. The Museum was still closed for the winter season, so I was enjoying a Sunday of freedom. I guess I was scaring Andrew because of what I was wearing, a neon yellow boa and baseball cap with black cat sunglasses. But I didn't care, I desperately need to have fun. Minutes before lining up, we demolished toasted ravs and mozzarella sticks.

"You'd better hurry up and munch those or I'll eat them all." He actually sounded concerned. I am starting to get my energy, appetite and my voice back. I devour what's left of the food.

Despite enjoying the atmosphere, I was still thinking about the move and how I should be packing. I found a place I was excited about and was getting ready to sign the lease.

We lined up along the parade route and I decided to go live on TikTok. "This is fun." For the next twenty minutes or so we wait for the hounds. Andrew is bored. I take selfies of us. When I see the pictures a year later, he seems absolutely bored. I notice that he's not happy at all.

The parade commenced and we immediately caught beads. I'm even one hand catching while shooting from my iPhone with the other. The floats are fun, the dogs are cute. I'm having a blast, Andrew is not. Our conversation dwindles.

"Let's go." Andrew whines. We leave when the parade is only about halfway over. "We can drive around and eat at La Bonne Bouche. It's a gorgeous day."

I'd planned to leave and nap after the parade and hoped that I'd be packing stuff by three or four in the afternoon. Instead, we head to west county.

"Have you been to Creve Coeur Lake? It's a gorgeous park?" I convince him. But as we drive in, he's not excited at all.

"Isn't the water gorgeous?" I muse as people are exercising, walking dogs and even picnicking nearby.

"Let's eat." Andrew didn't care about the park. I wonder how bad his depression has become and if he stopped his meds.

We arrive at Bouche and devour massive crème desserts. Their selection is incredible, pastries and cakes of various kinds. They even had Mardi Gras cookies. We sat at the window sipping fancy coffees and noshing our sweets. It's not long before he's scrolling and then asks me to shoot pictures.

Now I'm the one that's bored.

"Can you help me with a test? I'm near downtown." The desperation in Andrew's voice sounds like a soul seeking salvation. Andrew is still out of work.

I am absolutely bushed. I'm working three days a week at the antique shop, my gig working for the city is nearly up, plus I'm still filling in at the Museum. "Okay, come get me. I'd offer the apartment but there's shit everywhere and the Museum is open today with a bus tour, so meet me in the alley."

I have officially entered of an after phase of Covid where I'm a walking dead, my body somehow on autopilot, managing to go through the motions. Taking naps and still sleeping ten to twelve hours a night. I do not recommend getting Covid and having menopause simultaneously. I'm scared my hot flashes are fevers.

It was a sunny but chilly day better than it had been. We pulled over in Lafayette Park to take the test for a local jeweler management position on his phone.

"Would you read it aloud and I'll answer?"

"Yes." I hold his phone and begin. After the first questions, I can tell this is no ordinary entry exam. The test is quite simply, the examination version of hell. You reply to one question, then a few lines down, there's the same question, but phrased differently. There's four sections with twenty questions in each one. My post-Covid brain wants to die.

We slog along for about thirty minutes. Halfway through, we're picking random responses. Near the end Andrew totally checks out. "Just do it." He begs.

I finish it using my remaining communicating brain cells. He has no patience or focus. I'm out of fucks to give. He will fuck some guy after he drops me off at the Museum. He will not get this job, or any other he's applied for since he left the drug store and refuses to get back on meds. His resume is full of lies.

About a week later, Andrew texted that he's ending it all. I rushed over with food and prepared myself mentally to find his dead body. He surprisingly crawled out of his bedroom, disheveled and sleepy after taking too many Benadryl and probably drinking alcohol on top of it. "I didn't think you'd come."

I made tea and we eat in silence except that he demands a video of him drinking the tea. *I swear that this is the last time I do this for him.*

"Can you imagine what it would be like if we got that statue in here?" Andrew peers around the parlor. He's speaking of the statue that was sold in the estate auction and is now entombed at the mausoleum at Oak Grove.

Earlier in the evening we went to get a QuikTrip pizza and devoured it with hot chocolate bombs. We took dessert upstairs and ate on the rug in the parlor. I should be packing but agreed to a sendoff party.

"Are you coming back?" Andrew asked as I took the dividing ropes down and he examined a bunch of trinkets and fixtures.

"Not for a while. I have a lot to take care of. I want my weekends back, I'm burned out."

The old Andrew has returned spouting tasteless but charming double entendres and catty remarks. "They need to dust in here. What is this cheap crap on display for?"

We went upstairs to visit the bedrooms and the library where he fantasizes aloud about how Paris must have been at the time of the youngest Campbell son's stay.

"Are you going to miss it?" He sounds like he cares.

"The house? Yeah. And a lot of the volunteers. But not the work, it's a lot of responsibility. Mowing the lawn was getting rough." Covid left me so weak that I was glad I was leaving before the grass grew because I didn't think I'd be able to mow in that state.

We went downstairs, the air full of melancholy. We sat at the breakroom table. I don't even feel like talking at this point until he gasps.

"Did you see that?"

"What? You're joking. Stop it."

"No really, a dark shadow in the hallway." He made it sound like it was real but still joked, "It's Eliza!" Eliza was once an enslaved person who was granted her freedom and remained friends with the family.

"Shhhh! Are you serious?" I grab the dowsing rods. Andrew used to cajole that I was the latest slave at the Museum, often calling me Eliza in jest.

I am somewhat metaphysically gifted. I don't mind if you believe me or not. The Museum has always been haunted but the ghosts are friendly. I've had lots of experiences but that's a story for another time. I have a healthy respect for any spirits that might be lingering. So I jumped at the chance to see who was around that evening.

I begin to communicate, asking yes or no questions as the rods responded, moving side to side. Andrew is transfixed for a moment. In my six years in the Museum, I had a lot of ghostly contact but I'd never experienced anything with Eliza.

After about five minutes, the rods are moving slowly. Andrew walks away, bored and tinkering on his phone. I tell Eliza good night and put the rods away. The poor gal had to listen to his bullshit too. Asking me to communicate with the dead when I'm already tired, is a chore. I swear that she'll be an empathetic character in my book based on my experience at the Museum (I kept this promise, the *She Plays for Ghosts* eBook was released autumn of 2025).

"Let's go outside," Andrew suggests, "to take a final walk in the garden." We're not more than three steps into the yard when the lights came on in the cook's bedroom. This is another haunted phenomenon that spooks him. We don't stay in the yard much longer.

Andrew leaves without a lot of fanfare. I close up the house and I have to clean up. I have no energy to pack afterwards. He possessed that habit of sucking the last out of me.

15 A MOVE, A TORNADO & A LAST DRIVE

"Evil will never leave the house of one who pays back evil for good."
-Proverbs 24: 15-16

"Who did this book?" Andrew pulled a mock photo collection I made as a sample for a larger coffee table book. He never seemed to believe me when I told him how talented I was.

"Me. It's a book of my steampunk art."

I was broken at that point, mentally, physically, spiritually. March was the month from hell. Between moving from the Museum, working my temp job, working my new retail antique job and recovering from Covid still, I was a complete and utter mess. Moving just sucks.

There were multiple delays getting into my new apartment as they kept updating things before I moved in. Andrew didn't like my new space, but I loved it.

"Why you living in a beat up retirement community?" he grumbled. On trips back and forth he'd moan, "why didn't you get this place? Or this one?" as we drove past a wide variety of complexes.

"You know these are next to major roadways. Plus, two stories or more. Lots of noise and traffic. No thanks." I was happy with my choice.

I ended up moving to the area I grew up in. My new space was in my grandparents' old neighborhood in South County. It's single story rows of apartments. No one above or below, good neighbors, pleasantly quiet, and affordable.

We were packing up the remaining stuff in the carriage house apartment in the Museum. Earlier in the week most of my heavy furniture went out the window because of the narrow Victorian stairs. Everything needed to be off the carpet for the incoming cleaners. I ended up shoving stuff in the bathroom. I was out of time. I was exhausted. Not that I wasn't grateful for the staff and family that helped, but at one point, I couldn't even go back up the stairs to help with anything else. I was grateful that they finished the rest for me. I vowed I'd never do this again. I also hired additional movers for the last day. I was done.

"You have too much shit. You cannot live like this." Andrew griped as we packed and sorted. "Promise me you won't do this to your new space. I need to remind you that I don't want to be here."

I valiantly withheld my anger. I could remind him how I spent close to twenty hours cleaning and organizing his apartment. How he once promised me that we'd move in together and how many houses we looked at. How I helped him with his resume, finding work, and various other bullshit tasks he claimed he didn't know how to do. How he promised to pay me for random jobs and never did despite him being a trust fund baby. How he always used my phone to scroll on social media and check various selling sites and I answered scores of messages. All the times he absolutely had to have my full attention, then wasted it scrolling on his phone. How many times he was on the verge of committing suicide and I talked him down. How many times I told him I had to move, I needed to pack and he interrupted.

I know myself well, I have to plan in advance. He cut my packing and planning time to zero after it was already low from having Covid and overworking.

"Take this." I shove antiques at him including my grandfather's mantel clock that he bestowed to my uncle. "It's yours." I put aside donation items for the Museum. The additional movers came, I rented an extra temporary storage unit. I left around 11 p.m. I considered staying overnight, but there was nothing to eat and no bed. I also didn't want to mess up the carpet.

On the remaining day, I picked up Andrew out in St. Charles around 7:30 a.m. We grabbed a breakfast to go, hurried to St. Louis, packed, filled the van, drove and moved to the new apartment within ninety minutes by noon.

Andrew was pissed until he saw that the van was only half full and that wasn't even with stuff stacked up. "Oh, wow, you really didn't have that much stuff." He smiled. I wanted to slap his fucking face, but I was grateful for his help.

I took Andrew to a thank you brunch, took him to the Galleria to scout out the office where he had an interview later. When we arrived at the mall garage, I was too sore to get out of the car except to escape a killer fart he'd left behind.

"Too much dairy." He laughed as he popped out. I drove around with the windows down and the air on, as he searched for forty-five minutes inside the mall. I wondered if he had a hook up in a public restroom.

I drove him home, went to the Museum, emptied out the rest of the stuff to my car, dragged out more trash, distributed some things to the neighboring parking attendant and told him to check the alley later for anything he wanted. I cleaned for three to four hours before I left for South County at 1 a.m. I sat in the parking lot of my new place summoning the strength to walk to my new apartment. I was pissed at myself for putting things off, for not putting myself first, for putting up with Andrew's shit. I was embittered but too tired to even cry.

I redeemed myself. I gave away dozens of bags to charities. I sold a lot of stuff online. I have half of a small storage unit down from two. I eventually gave away almost everything Andrew gave me or that I bought whenever I was with him. I seriously think that the next thing I need to purge is him.

"We got nothing." Andrew texts a pic of him standing by his car in a light rain.

Two days before, the weather services were sending advance warnings of possible severe storms. The day of the storm I was keeping an eye on my phone. I'd been a spotter for the National Weather Service for over twenty years. 2025 had already been predicted to have similar meteorological makeup as 2011, a horrific year for massive tornadoes and deaths. I texted friends to be careful including Andrew.

“I don’t care where you are, get home.” I text. There are already bad storms north of the city as I leave for work in west county. We are texting for the next three hours. The severe weather gets pushed off to later in the evening, but a coworker and I are given permission to close the antique store an hour early. I can see the storms brewing in the west. I have elderly neighbors, I am yelling at them to get into their bathtubs, and I get out a flashlight and battery chargers.

The tornado sirens start going off around 8:15 p.m.

“I’m scared.” Andrew texts.

“Get in the bathroom. Get off the phone and charge it. You have a cell coming your way.” Between him and the neighbors I’m on texting wildly and watching the radar.

The sirens go off a second and third time. It has rained and hailed twice.

“I lost electricity.”

“Ugh, stay in the bathroom. And get off your phone.” *Stupid, no battery left on his old ass phone.*

“Okay.”

“I’ll text only if it’s important.”

He’s lucky, the storms up north were dying out, but have built to the south. The sirens go off a fourth and fifth time. By 10:15 p.m. it’s bad enough that I’m sheltering in my bathtub. The hail is falling so hard that it sounds like a dump truck is dropping a continuous pile of rocks on the roof. It hailed for close to seven minutes. My phone buzzed with a tornado warning on the radar app and I saw the signature hook of a tornado in Arnold, a city only a few miles away.

When it slowed to what sounded like only rain, I popped out for a peek. The temperature dropped and the grass was piled with white hail stones. A couple trees were ripped of huge branches, buildings lost some shingles and leaves were everywhere.

“I went out to my car to charge my phone. We didn’t get shit.” Andrew texted.

“I just avoided a tornado.” The sirens blared another round. “Be careful, but you should be in the clear.”

A half hour later he texted that the sky is clearing. Meanwhile the sirens were wailing for the eighth and ninth times. I was still concerned, keeping my phone charge and flashlight handy. We had two more smaller rounds of hail.

“My electricity is on! Going to bed.” Andrew messages.

“Good, you should be okay.” I pace and watch the news and social media as damage reports come in. It stopped raining heavily after midnight. As I finally fell asleep, I wondered why I should still be caring about Andrew.

“Oh, that was expensive.” Andrew peeked at my receipt from Golden Corral. We were on a couple last Sunday drives. I felt like I owed him another breakfast for the move. I was almost face down in the plates after finishing. I still didn’t have the best appetite and I’d rather been sleeping.

“Can we head to Pevely after we’re done? I’m invited to lunch. I need to find out how to get there.” Andrew smirked as he picked me up at my new place an hour before..

“Sure.”

“You want a popper?” He tugged what appeared to be an inhaler from his dash. I know I must’ve had the “what in the fuck?” look on my face because he next words were, “I picked it up at the gym, they’re legal.” He emitted a weird little laugh and took a quick hit as I shook my head no. He seemed pale, needed a shave and his baseball cap was nearly turned sideways off his head. I had a sick feeling that he was not anywhere near hitting rock bottom.

We finished feasting at the Corral and made our way down highway 55 towards Pevely.

"Have you ever been to Kimmswick? It's cool town."

"I think a long time ago?"

"We should do a drive through. It's full of historic homes and shops." But as we buzz around the quaint town, I can tell he's not into it.

"I can't wait for this brunch." He beams. This was to be a lunch for a select group of guests with a cultural benefactor at her family's property. Andrew asked, as he always did, if I'd be his plus one at the cottage soiree. Then it was reduced to just him and the donor, a wealthy kind woman. The plans evolved to nothing involving me as usual, one of his diluted adventures. "Can you help me find how to get there?"

"Yeah." It's a chilly day, sputtering flurries that phase into mist as we get to Pevely. I point out the softball fields and where the Teamster's Camp had been. "My dad took us when we were young. It was an amazing space. Great pool."

The address is not far off the highway. I pass it by accident and we turn around. "That's it." I pull off the side of the two-lane road as much as I can. "That's a long driveway."

"Ugh, you can't see the house from here," He mumbled. "Too bad. You know the Petring's owned this property for decades. I found one of the coffee cans and thought I'd donate it to the Museum. Anyhow, I'll get to see it later this week."

I am too tired to be envious.

"You want to hit up some bins?"

"Not downtown," I grumbled.

"No, here."

"Okay." As we're ready to leave Pevely I saw the sign for the local winery. "Oh, we have to stop." I do like my wine.

"Hmm, alright."

The winery is further away from the highway than I thought. We pass a couple of pockets of charming wealthy historic homes mixed alongside grand and petite farms. The winery itself is cute, including a dock and lake. It's packed with what looks like a wedding.

"Do you want to check it out?" I asked hesitantly.

"Nah."

I did not get my wine. We briefly stopped at the Goodwill near Arnold. We were barely there for ten minutes.

"Well, that was disappointing. I'm ready to go." Andrew had been scrolling as I was driving. He was in hook up mode. Within fifteen minutes, he dropped me off at my apartment.

"Yeah, I'm tired. I'm headed for a nap." I bounce out, not able to look at him.

"I'll text you later." He waved.

Whatever.

I do drink a lot of water and rest for about forty-five minutes. I rise to see a text.

"Hey, I need to see something. Can I swing by? I'll be there in ten minutes."

You have got to be fucking kidding me.

"Well, alright. You done getting laid?" *Why do I do this?*

He sends a devil snicker emoji.

Twenty minutes later we're off to the bins. Again. This time, it's downtown. I find a couple things including a small rug. He sorts out picture frames. I don't want anything. Ever. Again. Moving does that to you.

"You want to check out a few houses?" He's quasi excited.

"Sure." I can tell he's not in the mood, but he has to have some sort of afterglow I suppose. We ride aimlessly through the Central West End. We get drive-through and eat during the sunset in Forest Park. Although I am bored, I'm certain that we're in the ending of this pattern, eating or being in parks at sunset that have included Cliff Cave, Forest Park, Lafayette, and Whitecliff Park. As the glow of the sunset dwindled, so had this relationship.

One of the homes we passed that day had belonged to Jane Oaker. She too was a descendant of Andrew's, an Edwardian stage to film actress. Six weeks later, it would be destroyed by another tornado.

16 REVELATIONS

"The great dragon is thrown down, that ancient serpent, who is called the devil and Satan, the deceiver of the whole world."
-Revelation 12:9

I can make things very, very difficult for you. I opened my texts, somewhat relieved that I finally received a form of contact after Andrew ghosted me for several days. I was almost certain he committed suicide.

I was shocked at the completely brusque text. Even though it began with the phrase *This is not a threat...* it certainly was. The middle portion detailed that he was, in nutshell, going to tell anyone and everyone, anything I said about any of them, declaring that he had screen shots of proof and ended with *Also you have been blocked.*

I sat back, stunned at the brutality of the statement. I was so taken aback at this bizarre coercion tactic that I honestly asked if he intended it for me, that I held in confidence anything he told me, and forgave him for any past transgressions, meaning his outbursts and bad behavior.

About four short months later, I'd absolutely back out on this promise as I wasn't aware that he was a complete con artist and none of what he shared was true. Any salacious rumors he spread gave him a sort of sick satisfaction. He believed that he was a Truman Capote gossip hound. I didn't know it then, but a simple picture of Annie Lemp-Konta changed the course of my life forever and ended my friendship with Andrew.

I already felt this association grinding to a painful end for the past few months, and after the shock wore off, I was ready to walk away and let it die forever.

Roughly a week before this text exchange, I had sent him a screen shot of Annie's social media profile, from her Facebook page, run by one of her descendants. She came up as a suggested friend request and we had more than several mutuals on the social media app. In a wild twist, that relative of Annie's started that page ten years ago in order to expose Andrew's deceptions which were deep and prolific. I hadn't glanced at her page and hadn't the slightest idea of what was happening.

I sent him an invite to the member opening of the Roarin' 20's exhibition at the St. Louis Art Museum. Crickets. I didn't know what to think.

On March 30th I was invited to be a guest of honor at the Volunteer Party for the Museum. Another worker and I were retiring. That mid-afternoon another hailstorm blew through and I debated contacting Andrew and Abby to see if they might be going, as I waited for the storm to pass while I sat in the car.

No, I'm having fun. I bolstered myself into going alone. *This is about me, the staff and volunteers.*

I left for the party as soon as the hail stopped. I arrived at a packed wonderful event, purposely leaving my phone in my purse to enjoy the festivities. I'd forgotten about Andrew, until I needed a tissue and cough drop from my purse due to seasonal allergies.

I was shocked to see a missed text from Andrew asking if I was going to the volunteer party. I debated for a moment before responding that I'd missed his call. I'm not surprised that he didn't respond to my reply. A couple of people inquired where he was, I said he was working. In reality, I didn't know where he was and I was beginning not to care.

A couple days later, in early April, I confided in Abby that I hadn't heard from Andrew. I was concerned that he was suicidal again. After a short text exchange her answers became curt. She didn't want to get involved in anything in between Andrew and me. I wondered what the hell was going on. I decided not to worry about it, although I had the feeling something was still horribly off. I texted my friend Ethan to get the remaining bed pieces they owed to Andrew from last summer and sent his contact information. I didn't want to see anyone else get burnt.

About a week later, Abby texted that she hadn't heard anything from Andrew for over a week and was concerned. This was strange as she just said she didn't want to get involved. I told her I hadn't heard anything since our previous text. I shared he'd had several episodes where he'd said he'd commit suicide. As much as he pissed me off, I didn't want him to kill himself. Abby said with her medical credentials that she'd do a wellness check (in truth anyone can call on a wellness check if they know someone), but then Abby ended up having her husband call Andrew. And that Andrew was apparently okay.

I thought about the visceral twisted words he'd used to criticize and demoralize all kinds of people. This whole friendship was unhealthy. There was nothing left worth saving. I decided not to contact him. I kept the block up. He stopped following my social media. It was over. Or so I believed.

I was in the throes of setting up my apartment, beginning a new job and working my current contract with the city. I was getting enough sleep and feeling human at last. I was also starting to write and plan new book releases. I was moving on.

I still had Andrew's key, a suit jacket and coat I was altering for him and a rosary he gave me. It reminded me about how I spent an hour stitching on a MICDS school patch on a jacket for him as he was going to volunteer there. I went with my gut. I packed it all up and shipped it using tracking. I didn't even insert a note. I didn't tell him it was coming. I was done. I don't know what was wrong, but I wasn't dealing with any of this drama anymore. I couldn't put my finger on it, but things still weren't right.

My intuition was correct. After another couple of weeks passed, another odd text exchange from Abby saying that there's reports that I told people that she was able to take them on as clients for little or no cost. And that any word of this could jeopardize her career in the mental medical health field and filing for disability. Instantly I deducted that Andrew started something. I never offered her services to anyone. I only introduced her to Andrew to become friends and they seemed tight at the Holiday Parlor tours at the

Museum. I defended myself and took the high road even though I'd said nothing to anyone. Andrew was stirring the pot. I wasn't going to watch it boil.

Another week passed, another text from Abby, *Andrew got a job!* I ignored it and blocked her. If he was using her, or she was clinging to him, it was time to end any friendship including both of them.

I found out that my suspicions were right. Andrew was grooming Abby to be the next Margot. And for that brief month in April 2025, it was only the beginning of Andrew using Abby to check on me.

By the end of April, I was enjoying my new place and job. I was working regularly and simultaneously creating a new book based on my experiences with ghosts at the Museum and was planning an autumn book tour.

I was absently scrolling social media and Abby posted pics of her and Andrew together bookending lunch and dinner on a day that the Museum held its Members Party. His smile seemed more crooked the more he fell into the abyss of deception.

I know why she posted it, it wasn't for fun, it was click bait to get my attention, nudged on by him. This savvy fish didn't bite. I had other things to do. I ignored it.

I made a last contact. I felt like he should know that the May 17th tornado severely damaged the Central West End home one of his great-aunts, Jane Oaker, a St. Louis born Edwardian actress. I texted him a picture from the Post-Dispatch. There was no reply. I let any feelings die and focused on my artistic endeavors.

I'd been planning to start my own tea line that was based on my steampunk and vampire characters in my books, working with the London Tea Merchant on the subsequent blends that June. I began posting videos on social media using a "spilling the tea" promos. Spilling the tea ironically set off another series of stalking. Andrew thought my videos were about his secrets. Suddenly he and Abby were liking my posts on all my pages on TikTok. It was clear that they were keeping tabs. I ignored it…at first.

July turned into the month where the truth was be revealed. Right before the 4th of July holiday I had car issues. Help from friends and relatives got me to and from my job and the car fixed.

The very next day after my car died, Andrew texted (and copied Abby) "we were wondering if you were still alive." I was absolutely creeped out at this point. I wondered if they'd tampered with my car. I didn't reply.

Less than a week later, my part time job ended abruptly. Things hadn't been well at the antique store. I had the feeling that something was wrong there too. For the month of June, I filled in for several staff for various reasons but was then told that my hours would be cut. I was proactive and had already been searching for other work when I was dismissed. Something stuck in my head in those moments when I turned over my key. The owner said that I had claimed that I was a part of their family to customers. As I drove home that night, suspicions rose. Andrew had come into the shop for a couple visits to sell items. There was an instance that he was particularly unhappy with what he'd brought and left with. I couldn't prove it then, that Andrew was involved in my firing, but I'd soon learn that claiming to be a part of someone's family was a large portion of his charade. I don't think this was coincidence.

Two days later, I was at home job hunting when I received a phone call from a former employer. "Have you heard from Andrew lately?" That question opened a Pandora's Box of discoveries. Quite simply I was informed that Andrew Barringer was born Andrew Paulsen, a con artist. It wasn't hard to find proof once I had his birth name. I shook with anger as I investigated further. Andrew was never the person I thought he was.

The most damning evidence was a May 2015 article "The Last Lemp" by Jeannette Cooperman from St. Louis Magazine. That led to finding obituaries to finding living relatives to criminal records to multitudes of other people he'd scammed. On a smaller scale, there were those he simply lied to, and on a larger scale, profited off unapproved tours of the Lemp Mausoleum in Bellefontaine Cemetery to reselling antiques and vintage items he claimed belonged to the wealthy families of which he was never a part of, to spending a week with an older couple that lived in a historic home, Andrew claiming to be their relative. They threw him a thirtieth birthday party where he drank horrendously and reportedly vomited all over their home at the end.

He particularly liked to latch on to cultural institutions, (masking as a tour guide, volunteer, or highly interested visitor boasting of gilded descendants) the list of which reads like a Best of Historical St. Louis Guide: the Lemp Mansion, Chatillon DeMenil Mansion, Bellefontaine Cemetery, the Campbell House Museum, and Missouri Botanical Garden's Little Shop Around the Corner. He reached out to Oakland House to volunteer and was considering contacting the Hawken House and Sappington Houses before he was caught this round. He even went outside of St. Louis to the Pabst Mansion in Milwaukee in between his forays in St. Louis. He said he was a descendant of the famous brewing families there too. These smaller cultural and historical entities rely heavily on volunteers to keep them afloat. Andrew had done a lot of damage. It was a small comfort to know I wasn't the only victim.

The wildest fact in this whole charade is Andrew did this impostor act not just once, but twice, even after being discovered the first time in 2015.

I felt absolutely sick. There was no doubt in my mind that he used me to gain access to the Museum. Our Sunday drives were his way of collecting information about the famous families he claimed to be a part of, and using my social media to spy, stalk, and gain access to other people.

I can remember the first inklings of Andrew's stalking behavior. I was mowing the lawn for one of the final times at the Museum. It was an autumn Sunday sunny afternoon near sundown, the best period of the day to mow. Most of the pollinators, like bees and butterflies were winding down before the nighttime moths and rabbits came out. There would be shade from the building, but still enough light to mow. The challenge was to get it done before sunset. I could usually finish the whole mow, trim and blow off the walkways within ninety minutes. It was one of the last nice days when I had time available to do the work. I was driven to get it finished and get a decent bath or shower in after.

Mowing is dirty business. The yard is immense, wrapping around the front and side of the house and extending to an upper and lower plots of grass. Also, I needed to allot for time to gas up the mower, load the trimmer, add batteries to the equipment and gear up. I have some seasonal allergies and don't like sunburn, so I wore a long sleeve shirt with a tee shirt, long pants sometimes layered with shorts for pockets (for my phone and keys), boots, thick socks, gloves, a hat, sunglasses and a mask to cover my nose and mouth (I did this even before Covid to protect my face). I'd throw in a bandanna and water nearby.

I managed the Museum that afternoon for tours. Andrew texted that he wanted to head out for a drive as I was working. I replied that I had to mow first and I wouldn't finish until near 7 p.m. It seems like he never took my duties seriously.

The minute the Museum was locked up, I ran over to the carriage house, changed into work clothes and got started. When I was mowing, the world could end and I probably wouldn't notice. It's loud and even with my phone on vibrate or loud as it'll go, I can't hear a thing. To get the job done quickly, my mind went into a dreamy kind of autopilot mode where I followed a strict method and pattern.

I was roughly five minutes from completing it, when I looked up to see Andrew waiting at the side gate, waiving wildly to get my attention. I yelled for him to wait as I couldn't shut off the mower and hurried to wrap it up. I finished and scurried to let him in the yard.

"I called and called your cell. Then I tried the Museum line. Did you want to get a pizza?" He seemed agitated and jumpy.

"Yeah, but I have to clean up first." I am absolutely filthy and sweaty. I'm also tired and irritated. I'd really rather relax than entertain him that evening.

"You look pretty butch." He snorts with laughter. "Just wear what you have on."

I try not to be pissed. For a gay person he certainly likes to use a lot of slurs. And although I'm straight, I still find it insulting that he implies that a woman, whether straight, gay or trans, can't be feminine and still mow the yard like a boss. Protecting oneself from the elements is essential no matter who you are.

"You'll need to wait outside." I hustled to get the yard equipment into the cellar. I became increasingly agitated as I locked up the Museum then rushed up to the apartment to grab my purse, at least wipe my face, and hit the bathroom. I'm gross, hair matted, sticky and I can't even imagine how I might smell. I made a feeble attempt to spray down using body mist.

I dashed downstairs and we walked to his car. We left for QuikTrip, picked up drinks and a pizza to go and returned to the Museum. I wondered *why in the hell did he have to have to have my attention*, especially since he was on the phone the whole time, endlessly scrolling for a hook up or antiques. By the time he left after eight, I'm exhausted and hating myself for bending to him.

In hindsight, I am grateful that Covid kept me away from him so I could see his issues more clearly. I was no longer equipped to assist him with his mental disorders. I couldn't take care of him without neglecting myself. I was not falling on that sword any longer. He threw his attention to Abby thinking it could make me jealous. She'd drown in the wake of his deceptions or figure it out like everyone else. This whole debacle was not my circus, not my monkeys. I blocked them from my social media. I moved on.

By August I was focused on producing books, finding new employment, and preparing for the Bump in the Night Book Tour with a friend.

I was excited to be exploring one of my characters further. A few years ago, as we were coming out of the pandemic I came up with Stella, a three-hundred-year old cougar vampire assassin character with a repressed memory…that starts to remember.

Please humor me for a creative process moment. I already used social media to create book trailers since 2013. TikTok, with its unique filters and algorithm took that creativity to a whole new level. I'd save money and use my own abilities to be Stella. Making short films and books became a paradise of artistic expression for me. Stella has her own TikTok page and four books (as of this first publication) with five more works in progress.

In mid-July 2025, I received a "last text to mend fences" from he and Abby, claiming that I abused their friendship, used them and that I exhibited delusions of grandeur, pretending to be a Countess, really an odd statement.

It was pure nonsense to stop my books and creativity, to create a distraction. Like many who propagate these kinds of crimes, they do it to create shame or fear in their victims, the entrapment phase.

I didn't bite. I've had the Countess moniker since 2012 and had trademarked it, with books and products already under its brand umbrella. I've been a practicing author and artist over forty years. I've indie published over thirty books and short stories with a few Amazon best-sellers and have made St. Louis Magazine's A-List. I've won arts awards, grants and public art projects. I found it humorous that a bi-polar impostor was calling me crazy.

I didn't bother answering the text. Why they were making an odd effort to text me after months of no contact and blocking me? Quite simply, it was a fishing expedition. At this point, I was done with the shenanigans. Friends suggested that I should write a book about this whole mess. I agreed and made a simple post announcing on social media that 2025 was a rough year and I was writing a book about the experience and that the loose leaf teas based on my book characters were coming online.

A week or two passed and another phone call from the previous employer. Andrew claimed I was running a smear campaign against the Museum. Of course I wasn't. We both agreed that there was nothing wrong with that particular video and I'd remove it. But I also noted that Andrew wouldn't stop and as in past developments, I was right. I consulted an attorney and continued to collect texts and note conversations thoroughly should things go violently sideways and I'd need to file a restraining order. After all, he had owned assault rifles at one time.

At that point I was just sick of it all. I vowed to exorcise this demon and moved on. I came up with the title of this book and set everything having to do with Andrew aside. This story would be written at another moment when I could give it the attention it deserved.

17 AFTER LUCIFER HAD FALLEN

"I saw Satan fall like lightning from heaven."
-Luke 10: 18

"I'm gonna fuck Christopher Rice," Andrew boldly declared. It was almost a year before everyone found out his second round grift, Autumn 2024, and we had planned a vacation to New Orleans. I celebrated the whole month of October, but 2024 fell flat. I said I'd do things differently the next year. I did what I said.

2025 would be about Halloween in NOLA. Anne Rice's son, Christopher Rice, and longtime friend and fellow author Eric Shaw Quinn were doing a Celebration of Life on November 1st, All Saints Day. Initially it was a large group traveling: me, Andrew, Abby, two best friends from college, my longest, best friend since childhood, and another creative friend and possibly her daughter. Andrew was convinced that somehow he was going to seduce Christopher Rice on our trip.

As the drama progressed and everyone else backed out for various reasons, I bought two tickets to an event I wasn't sure I was going to. But thanks to the generosity of my aunt, I traveled to New Orleans for Halloween in the French Quarter and the Anne Rice Celebration of Life.

I cancelled the other normal October "fun" plans. I already lined up a mini book tour with a friend that authored a fantastic book on St. Louis Haunted History. I promoted *She Plays for Ghosts*. Together we did our Bump in the

Night book tour that kicked off with a bucket list lecture at the Central Library in Downtown St. Louis. Each stop was a lot of fun and successful in its own way.

NOLA was the cherry on top of Halloween season, an absolute dream of a much needed vacation. I wasn't sharing pics on social, at first. I didn't want to hear any crap from Andrew or Abby. I changed my mind, I didn't care, I wasn't letting their hate steal my joy. We shared like crazy, including a stop in Sikeston, MO for throwed rolls at Lambert's. Halloween on Bourbon Street was insane as we enjoyed blood bags at the Vampire Cafe. The botanical gardens beautiful. The Anne Rice Celebration of Life was touching and sweet. We waited for close to four hours to meet Christopher Rice, but it was an amazing once in a lifetime experience. He and Eric Shaw Quinn were incredibly kind. I came away so inspired. We ate tons of delicious food, from Café du Monde to The Apothecary to Acme Seafood. Add on a visit to the Rice crypt and historic graves at Metairie Cemetery, the unique shops, art galleries and petite spaces spread over the French Quarter. NOLA was the excursion I needed to heal my wounded soul.

Despite a small virus on the ride home, I returned to St. Louis invigorated and excited. I finished Stella's third book and began the fourth. My new job was fun and creative.

Near Christmas I was promoting events. I hadn't been on Substack for at least two months and noticed that Abby had been following me, probably at the behest of Andrew. There since right before my visit to New Orleans and after, still stalking. I blocked them from one additional social media post. I figured once this book promo campaign commenced, they'd probably start stalking again anyway. Let them see. I had nothing to hide.

I pitied Abby. She was another Margot who was used to make inroads for him. How she continued to believe his bullshit even after she had access to the St. Louis Magazine article from 2015 was beyond me.

I began researching for more background on the book. I contacted one of the Lemp relatives that had been scammed. Updates were posted on their Facebook page. Once I became acquaintances with one of the extended Lemp family members, it was as if I'd opened the keys to the kingdom. People that clashed with or were victimized by Andrew previously came out of the woodwork. Volunteers and staff from various institutions. Ex lovers or dating prospects from hook up apps. Other women who were his "Margot" sidekicks who didn't know about his past until he disappeared when the truth arrived.

His MO was the same, especially with older females. Friend them through an intense amount of texts and calls (one described it as "love bombing") get close quickly, know everything about them, make offers and promises (move "in with me," "let's go to such and such") and then when the truth was discovered, instant ghosting or threats to harm their reputations. His constant texts when we were hanging out were to other people he was playing, either women he was using for contacts, access, or men he was hooking up with. And true to pattern, every few months as I wrote and did pre-promotions for this book, he'd send a threatening email.

The similarities were uncanny. The people I spoke with experienced the same hell, pulled in with flattery, then attempted aligning with catty, condescending criticisms that left them feeling embittered and icky. Another volunteer felt like she was "…groomed through constant contact. Then he wanted your undivided attention as he distracted himself on his phone. And when you found out about his past? Complete ghosting, blocking. Then a strange 'hi' text months later, a level of insane gaslighting." Of course we'd all have moved on by then, flabbergasted at the weirdness of it all.

"He wanted to do nice things for others on your dime, like throwing a party but suddenly you were footing the bill or it went on without you," another former friend said. It immediately reminded me of how he wanted to throw a birthday party for Abby and "would I be able to cook? Maybe rent a venue?" Fortunately, I was working a lot and preparing to move, so I at least I didn't get drawn in that particular time.

Men he dated and coworkers had similar strange experiences. How Andrew managed to hold onto any job was a complete mystery. He purposely targeted smaller institutions like historic house museums to perpetuate his charade. Most had limited staff and resources but still found out about his false past. St. Louis is a little big town. Word gets around fast.

So many truths came to being. His mother, running the red light in Ladue, it wasn't in the tony suburb of West County, but a small town in central Illinois outside of Bloomington. They never owned a limo, let alone a driver. His father died several years before, and both parents pasts were fairly checkered. I could go into much more detail, but in a nutshell, the fruit didn't fall from the tree, and this is about Andrew. He is ultimately responsible for his bullshit.

He trolled historical and cultural institutions, famous families, gay dating and hook up apps for his numerous victims, using his charm and faux connections to gain items for resale at the least. At the most, he reportedly threatened to burn down another victim's house. He seemed to know the exact millimeter of the line that could be crossed legally without getting arrested.

In good conscience, I could not keep most of what he gave me. I will always wonder how much of it was inappropriately pilfered. Did he feign ignorance so I'd fill in the details that he'd use for his own deceptive fantasies later? I wonder if he conned his way into the Antiques Road Show.

After we found the Petring plot in Bellefontaine, I remember how he joked that we'd be buried together so he could tease me into eternity. I shudder in horror as I'm writing this ending chapter, exactly a year to the date that we went searching. The more I found out about him, the more I pitied him.

Andrew had an innate fear and hatred of himself. I remember him sending pics of possible outfits for a job interview. When I told him they all looked great (which they did) and he looked attractive, he got weirdly angry. Note there was no romantic love here, just kindness. It's unfortunate that he weaponized it amongst the people who cared the most.

With additional solid research, I have more than enough dirt for a sequel. I'd bury him. But my other muses are calling for now, and they are a lot more pleasant. Writing this was literally akin to exorcising a demon. Emotions that I buried resurfaced enough to make me walk away from the laptop more than once to maintain my sanity.

I am a totally different person. I hated who I'd become when I was around Andrew. Stella's got her groove back, literally. I wrote two more Vermilion Countess books, released another stand alone, and finished an omnibus for another vampire series in the last year with five other works in progress and a major relaunch of my catalog. I learned to stop blaming myself for being in the bubble of managing to survive Covid, moving, and changing jobs five times in eighteen months. He thought I'd be hurt, that I wasn't his 'pick me girl' anymore, that I'd be afraid. He was wrong.

My current employers are well aware of who Andrew is. I have confirmation that he did contact at least one of them with deprecating false information about me.

This is especially ironic, as he's supposed to be currently working for a high end designer jewelry company known for their silver. That too is a lie. He was born Andrew Paulsen, but claimed to be a Lemp, a Pabst, a Pullman, a Petring, a Niedringhaus, and a Donahue/Woolworth, and has gone by DeVille and Barringer. I'm sure there's more that I've missed at the time of this publication.

Andrew threatened to make my life very, very difficult, and he did—for a little while. The truth came out and his past caught up to him, again. I can't imagine he'll be in St. Louis much longer if he's still here.

I'd suppose that Andrew's biggest fault was he didn't believe any of my stories. Although they are pretty crazy, my life has been an adventure, and my tales are true. I do know a lot of people, but I never abused my ability to network and assist others. I didn't ask for favors or steal. My family lineage is legit. His lack of belief is ironic considering the scope of his lies.

I was ready to let it go. I mentally prepared myself to walk away from the drama. But he poked the bear one time too many. Mama bear didn't get angry, she got even. You might ask why write this? Because he's still out there, and who knows who he is pretending to be.

I almost sent Andrew a copy of this inscribed "Read it and weep, bitch," but I thought that his cheap ass should buy his own copy. I smile when I remember that Andrew wanted to be immortalized in my books. Now he is, at least in this one.

"Lucifer left me when a late frost killed the early spring,
I told the trees and conversed with the crows about what he had done.
They sent angels and guardians to surround in a ring,
And through perseverance and truth, a written victory was won."

-"Lucifer Fallen," Victoria L. Szulc

ABOUT THE AUTHOR

Victoria L. Szulc is a multi-media artist and author, a Renaissance woman living a gothic Steampunk life, The Countess®. She "lives" her art, loves to draw, specializing in pet portraiture and other artistic endeavors through her company The Haute Hen™. Victoria is an experienced weather spotter for the NWS, a history nerd, adores things that go bump in the night, and appreciates a strong sweet cup of tea.

OTHER WORKS BY VICTORIA L. SZULC

More works (and future releases) by Victoria L. Szulc:

The Society Trilogy (Steampunk Gothic Romance Adventure):
Book 1-Strax and the Widow
Book 2-Revenge and Machinery
Book 3-From Lafayette to London

More Society Steampunk Stories (Steampunk Gothic Romance Adventure):
A Long Reign, The Society Travelers Series, v.1
The Kicho, The Dolls of Society, v.1
A Dream of Emerald Skies, A Young Society Series, v.1

The Brown Lady, Short Story Edition

She Plays for Ghosts (Gothic Paranormal Romance)

The Vampire's Little Black Book Series (Gothic Dark Romance Series)

The Vermilion Countess Series (Gothic Dark Romance Series)

A Book of Sleepy Dogs (Fine Art Dog Portraiture)

www.ingramcontent.com/pod-product-compliance
Lightning Source LLC
Chambersburg PA
CBHW061537050726
47593CB00002B/816

* 9 7 8 1 9 5 8 7 6 0 4 6 8 *